THE INTERLOPER

DEBESH BANERJEE

INDIA • SINGAPORE • MALAYSIA

Copyright © Debesh Banerjee 2024
All Rights Reserved.

ISBN 979-8-89446-369-8

This book has been published with all efforts taken to make the material error-free after the consent of the author. However, the author and the publisher do not assume and hereby disclaim any liability to any party for any loss, damage, or disruption caused by errors or omissions, whether such errors or omissions result from negligence, accident, or any other cause.

While every effort has been made to avoid any mistake or omission, this publication is being sold on the condition and understanding that neither the author nor the publishers or printers would be liable in any manner to any person by reason of any mistake or omission in this publication or for any action taken or omitted to be taken or advice rendered or accepted on the basis of this work. For any defect in printing or binding the publishers will be liable only to replace the defective copy by another copy of this work then available.

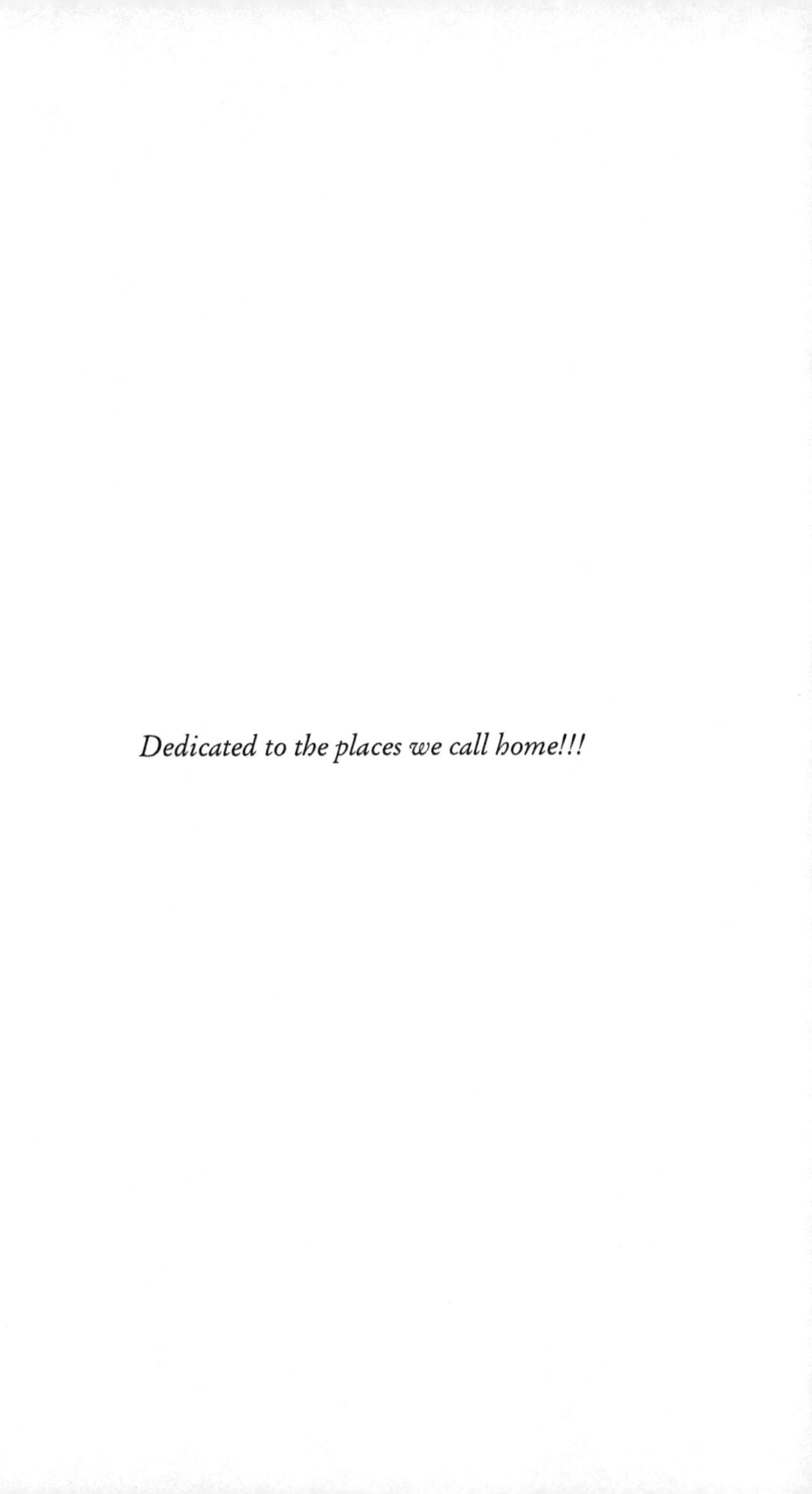

Dedicated to the places we call home!!!

Contents

Acknowledgement

It took me almost ten years to complete this work, so it is apt to say that the story and the narrative has evolved and grown with me. As such, every person who has played a role in shaping up my life over these past years deserves to be credited for their contribution. However, since that is an impossible task, here are the ones who deserve special mention –

My friends who always stood by me and supported my dreams, even though they might have seemed unrealistic and foolish.

My editor Varsha Naik whose guidance and inputs have enriched the story and shaped it into its best version.

My wife Anupriya who is my most trusted critique and sounding board for my most audacious ideas.

Lastly, my heartfelt gratitude to the people of Bengal, whose lives and times have inspired this story.

The **Journey**

The year was 2004. It was a warm and cloudy Saturday afternoon. A rickety bus painted in obnoxiously loud shades of red and green came to a blaring halt at the Swarajnagar junction on NH16. The visibly shabby vehicle had its name printed on its side – "The Royal Bengal". It was delayed by more than an hour, but that was pretty much its usual routine. People who depended on it for their daily commute were used to the fact. In fact, they planned their schedule accordingly. If someday the bus happened to arrive on time, it might actually prove inconvenient for them.

And the reasons for its delay were almost always the same – expected traffic congestion near the new Natunpur market, an almost stoppage near the railway gate at Poltonchawk, followed by a random detour due to ongoing construction work between Churua and Madhuganj. The pitiful condition of the road for the most part of the journey turned it a bumpy joyride, sans the joy. However, it became slightly bearable upon reaching the highway which lead all the way up to the eastern shores of India. It served as a life line for the people who lived along its stretch. Swarajnagar happened to be one of the oldest settlements in the area, apart from being the busiest one. It overlooked half a dozen villages scattered in a twenty-kilometre radius.

Despite its rich history, Swarajnagar was now a pale memory of what it once was. Situated along the edge of urban Bengal, it was surrounded by little known places and inhabited by even lesser-known people. Once you reach there, it felt like one of those places that had got lost somewhere in time. It was once meant for something big, and now it barely exists. And while it had visibly fallen far behind in the race, yet somehow it refuses to lose hope – hope of a better future for the generations to come. It tries to replicate and imitate the society that they wish to become, while its ethnic values continue to tear it apart. A lazy stroll down the dusty alleys and narrow lanes will transport you to the realms of a bygone era. You would get to see temples dating back centuries, which now lay in ruins; the dry and empty bed of a once-mighty river that had changed its course over time, and maybe an abandoned factory with rusted machinery still waiting for its gates to open since 1947. You would also hear about martyrs and heroes – young men, local lads, who had spilt their blood fighting tyranny and oppression. They belong to different chapters in time, their struggles differ in context. The names of the fallen ones remain etched in people's memory. Their lives have become tales now, and it is no longer possible to distinguish facts from fiction. To a stranger, this would seem to be a place caught in a time warp, where all the things irrelevant and obsolete is carefully preserved, loathing in the essence of a decaying greatness that no longer exists.

Coming back to the present, a total of three people alighted from the bus at Swarajnagar. One among them was visibly the odd one out. He was a young man – thin, fair, with long unkempt hair and sporting old-school reading glasses. He wore a loose white shirt, a faded pair of jeans, and carried a huge backpack on his shoulder. It was an exceptionally hot and humid day, and he looked exhausted. It was obvious that he was not from these parts and neither seemed used to the rigorous perils of travelling. He stood there for a while, stretching his limbs as far as they would go. Then he pulled out a folded sheet of paper from his back pocket, now moist with sweat and dirty along the folds. He opened it with extreme care and narrowed his eyes, trying hard to read something off it. It was a map, a political map to be precise, of the district. A red, dotted line ran across the map, right up to the border on the right. He carefully studied the map for a minute and then folded it and put it back in his pocket. It was evident from his expression that the map had not been of much help and so, he needed to other means to find his way ahead.

He looked around – the bus stop bore a sorry look. There were a few small shops and a shabby terminal for the passengers. Among the shops, which were barely shanties, were a stationary outlet, a food stall, and a bicycle repairing place. The boy pondered upon his options for a minute and then, having made up his mind, walked into the restaurant, if it could be so called. It reminded the boy of how hungry he was. All he had for breakfast was a sandwich while leaving home, but that seemed a long time ago, and his stomach had started to make rumbling noises. It had taken him about six and a half hours to reach Swarajnagar, and the journey had been rather arduous given that it was just about two-hundreds of kilometres from Kolkata. His mother had insisted on packing him some lunch for the road when he left. But in his desperate bid to exhibit self-reliance, he had outright refused the offer – a decision he now regretted. His father, however, had completely ignored him even as he left, but that was usual for him. He was well aware that his father considered doing anything without a prospect of profit as sheer waste of a man's time. He also knew that his father's indifference was the least of his worries, and he would have to be prepared to face a lot worse if he chose to continue along his intended path.

The restaurant was called "Annapurna Cabin". It was a small hut no bigger than a room, hosting a few wooden benches and tables, occupied by shabbily dressed people having a meagre meal. A grey-haired gentleman sat behind a desk near the entrance, attending to the customers and passing their orders to a couple of young boys he employed. They all spoke in impeccable native

Bangaal dialect, which even urban Bengalis would find tough to understand. The menu was scribbled on a blackboard that hung behind the desk. They served everyday food at a rate affordable by people who frequented this place.

"We also serve delicacies during festivals. That time you will get Hilsa, prawn, mutton – everything," the man behind the desk spoke as he saw the boy reading the rather short list with disappointing eyes. "Irrespective of what you order, we will serve it hot and tasty," he insisted confidently while sporting a hearty smile. Albeit sceptically, the boy ordered a full vegetarian meal. A kid quickly came and cleared a table for him to sit while he eyed the food on others' plates. It smelled good, and it fuelled his hunger all the more.

Twenty minutes later, he finished his lunch, having taken an extra helping of almost every item. Happy and full, he walked up to the gentleman at the counter to pay the bill. He seemed to be a nice person, humble and friendly. He had already checked on him twice while he ate and ensured that he got the best possible service from the attendants.

It was obvious that the gentleman loved to talk. It could be about anything, as long as the other person continued to respond. As the boy approached the counter, he could sense that the man was eager to start a conversation. He was greeted with a cheerful grin, followed by the statutory question, "I hope you liked the food, right?"

It was more of a statement disguised as a question, so the boy smiled, with a slight nod of his head.

He wanted to avoid any further banter. But it took him a couple of minutes to get hold of his wallet from his backpack, and the gentleman made full use of the window to slip in another comment. "You don't seem to be from around these parts. So, may I ask what work brings you here? I am sure nobody would come here for leisure!" He smiled as he unleashed his barrage upon him.

To be fair to the man, his curiosity was called for. Outsiders seldom came along this way, unless they have very specific purpose. And the boy definitely looked like an outsider – his appearance warranted these queries. And though he usually preferred to avoid casual banter with strangers, this time around it presented him with a welcome opportunity. It was getting late, and this man seemed just the right person to help him out. Whether he would choose to do so or not was, of course, a different matter altogether.

"Here you go, mister. Count it if you want to," the man continued to speak with the same fervour as he handed over the change to the boy.

"That wouldn't be necessary, Uncle, I am sure you would have checked," the boy replied with an equally broad smile, instantly striking a chord with him. "In fact, I wanted to thank you for the delicious food. I almost didn't expect it when I started from home," he cajoled, but in absolute honesty.

The man's smile broadened at the compliment. "Do you mind telling me your name, son?" he asked politely.

"Not at all uncle. My name is Nando Kumar Ghosh; you can call me Nando if you please" the boy responded with a slight bow, as a mark of respect for the elder questioner.

The man greeted him back with folded hands as he introduced himself, "everybody around here calls me Das babu, and I have grown so used to it that anything else comes as a surprise. But I guess you should be calling me uncle only and nothing else. After all, how old will you be? Twenty-one maybe, or twenty-two?" The man looked at him inquisitively as Nando grinned and nodded his head. And then he continued "it was long before you were born, when my wife and I came here from across the border, from East Pakistan. We managed to escape with our lives, unlike many of my folks. So many died, all over a small piece of land, which was once India, then Pakistan, and now, Bangladesh." The man continued to smile as he spoke, but his eyes were ridden with pain. "That day when we came here, we had nothing. All that we prayed for was some food. God has been kind, and so we live to tell the tale. But that day, I decided, if I was going to do something for a living, I would be making food. You know, I still get all my vegetables freshly delivered by the farmers every morning." He then started detailing the amount of effort that goes into keeping up the quality of his food, when Nando decided to interrupt him. "Uncle, I am in a bit of problem here. I am supposed to reach Damanpur by sundown, but my bus arrived late. I don't know what to do. Can you please help me out?" he asked with a sorry face, trying to garner his sympathy.

"Damanpur!" Das exclaimed with utter surprise, and for a moment it seemed he again had questions cropping up in his mind, but he refrained from asking them. Instead, he responded with a hearty smile, "I am afraid that won't be easy, my son, especially at this time and given the circumstances. But since you have come this far, let me see what I can do for you." Saying so, he left his desk and disappeared behind a door at the back of the room. Nando didn't enquire any further about the "circumstances" the man was referring to. Had he done that, his future could have taken a different course. But destiny had something else in store, and so, his stream of thoughts led him elsewhere.

Nando was expecting a suggestion at best, but he definitely didn't expect the man to empty his seat and go out looking for help. Nando believed that going the extra mile to help a stranger was a virtue that no longer existed. In fact, if somebody did that today, it would be relatively safe to assume that the person eyed some form of benefit from it. Nando felt alarmed. Nando was a mere hundred miles away from home and yet, the terrain felt unknown, and people seemed unreliable. He would probably have been more comfortable in a city like Bangalore or Hyderabad, where people speak a different language and eat different food. Or, for that matter, even in Sydney or New York, where they use a different currency or drive along the other side of the road. He could relate more to those places than to this neighbourhood because no matter how far these places are or how different their culture is – their core is made of concrete. The roads, the machines, their clothes, their hobbies – they all mimic each other. You can hop into a cab, or watch a movie, or climb in an elevator. Compared to that, this place seemed alien, and the differences, astronomical.

After waiting for no more than five minutes, Nando had already made up his mind to leave the place quietly. And as if almost on cue, that's when Das babu returned, but this time from the front of the shop. Obviously, there must have been a way of getting around the shop from behind, but Nando was visibly startled to see him there. Das babu gauged the situation immediately and broke into laughter, much to Nando's embarrassment.

"Don't worry, come with me," he told Nando in an assuring tone and started walking. Nando noticed that Das babu too was now carrying a bag with him. It seemed quite heavy and the sun was beating down, but Das babu looked like he was strolling in the park on a winter afternoon. Nando on the other hand struggled to keep up with him with his luggage. They walked along the highway for another hundred yards, and then turned left, leading down a slope into a square plot of land littered with humus and dung. It was a local farmer's market, which opened for business once every week. For the rest of the week, it would offer a sumptuous buffet of organic waste for the animals. The ground below looked like mud cakes, with bits and pieces of rock jutting out of it. Nando could only imagine what a nuisance the place would become when it rained.

They entered a narrow lane at the other end, about ten feet wide, that lead to a forking junction, which divided the path into two different ways. Trees and bushes closely enveloped these tracks, blocking the view ahead. At this intersection stood a solitary rickshaw van, with a huge black umbrella tied to a pole stuck at the back of the driver's seat. Under its shade sat a stout, dark man, smoking a *beedi* while fanning himself with a piece of cloth. The arm that held the smoke rested on the knee on which he squatted, while the other leg hung loosely from the side of the carriage. He wore a sooty T-shirt over a chequered *lungi*, and his unkempt stubble made it impossible to guess his age. Everything about him, from his posture to his expression, oozed a candid reluctance to all the earthly matters.

However, his demeanour changed as soon as the man caught sight of them. He threw away the *beedi* and jumped off his van, greeting Das babu with an awkward salute and slight bow of his head. He then noticed Nando, and in spite of being visibly surprised at this unexpected company, the men chose to ignore Nando for the next couple of minutes as they engaged in an animated conversation a few metres away from him. Das babu handed over the bag he was carrying to the other man, who passed a quick glance inside to check its contents, and then with a slight nod of acknowledgement, hung it beneath the van. The man was now ready to depart, to deliver whatever the package contained to wherever it needed to be. It was then that Das babu pointed towards Nando and said something to the man, to which the latter reacted a bit hesitantly. Then they both turned and looked at him, and he greeted them with a sheepish grin. He was sure that they were discussing about his transportation. He now looked at the van once again. He had seen vehicles like this before, and he knew for a fact that it is a common mode of transport in many parts of India. Nando had seen videos and pictures of people travelling in them along with vegetables, utensils, and sometimes even cattle. But now, as the realisation dawned upon him that he was about to experience it first hand, he didn't find it as exciting as he thought he would. Das babu was still busy trying to convince the man. Nando tried hard to eavesdrop on their conversation, but all he could figure out was the man's apparent displeasure and his frown upon the mention of Damanpur. But since they both spoke in their native dialect that Nando found hard to understand, he remained clueless about the reason behind it. A few seconds later, Das babu called him closer. "This is Horen" he uttered as he tapped the man on his shoulder. Nando smiled and nodded his head in greeting. In return, Horen too responded with a gentle nod and wry smile, even as he continued to check him out from the top to the bottom.

"He will take you there safely, don't you worry, young man" Das babu assured Nando once again as he boarded the van. Nando thanked him, still wary of his doubts as he prepared to leave. Horen had picked up his bag and was already in the driver's seat. As he pushed the paddle, Nando turned back and waved his hand to Das babu, who waved back at him with a calm and hearty smile. However, as he unconsciously turned around once again a moment later, Nando noticed him still standing there, hands folded in prayer and touching his forehead as he looked up at the sky. Nando knew this gesture – his mother would do the same when she felt her boy was headed for trouble.

* * * * *

The **Turbulence**

Half an hour later, they were still tottering along the pitted paths of the village on that wobbly rickshaw van. And Horen predicted it would take at least an hour more to reach Damanpur high school where Nando was headed. They could have reached sooner, but Horen had to take multiple detours along the way, to ferry stuff that people had entrusted him to collect and deliver. That is what he did for a living. It was sheer coincidence that he needed to drop something at Damanpur that day, and so he had agreed to take Nando along. Nando, however, was pleasantly surprised as he got to know the man up close. He was nothing like what Nando had imagined when he first saw him. On the contrary, Horen turned out to be quite a jovial and boisterous fellow, and commanded the love and respect of the local people. He proactively became a tour guide for Nando. He insisted that Nando sat squatting on his haunches with his legs crossed in front of him, instead of letting them dangle by the side of the van as he would have preferred. This way, he would avoid hitting something by the roadside and at the same time avoid a painful swollen feet due to improper blood circulation. Nando was grateful for this suggestion. The van didn't seem so uncomfortable after that, as he sat perched on top of it, gaping at the sombre beauty of the countryside.

Everything around was predominantly brown. Still safe from the concrete invasion, the atmosphere smelled like good old earth. The road below was just mud and bricks, and so were the walls of the huts that lined along its edges. The roofs were either thatched with straw or shabby, slippery tiles. Almost every home had some open space with plants around it. Even the water in the ponds looked green, as it mirrored its surroundings. Nando felt that if he had a bird's eye view, the entire landscape would look like a mundane montage of brown and green basking in the dying rays of the setting sun. The only things adding variety to these dichromatic surroundings were the different kinds of flowers that bloomed in abundance in every nook and corner. Their names were as novel as their distinct aromas that filled the air. Not all smells are good or bad; some are just refreshingly different. These were of that kind.

There were almost as many cattle as there were people, and they travelled the roads like it belonged to them. Twice during the journey, Horen had to steer his way through a herd of cows, and he did so with the precision of a surgeon, ensuring that neither the animals nor his passenger got hurt. The animals were covered in mud and dirt, but for the people around, they were a precious part of their lives. The women fiddled with cow dung with their bare hands as if it was fresh cream. They will use it to make dung cakes for fuel and would swipe their floors with it to keep evil spirits away. Their kids would happily play around in the cattle shed all day long.

Along their way, they crossed big temples with large wooden gates and big brass bells hanging from their roofs. And then they crossed small shrines by the road, housing nothing but a round piece of rock smeared in oil and vermillion. Huge stacks of hay dotted the vast open fields at regular intervals. Shabbily dressed kids chased the van, giggling to their heart's content for no good reason. The visual of an urban teenager riding atop a rickshaw van provided a circus show for them, delivered to their doorsteps. But there was no sarcasm in their smiles – it exuded nothing but a genuine and childlike happiness. Wherever they stopped, people greeted them with warmth and offered them water and sugar. They would smilingly pose for Nando's camera as he attempted to capture scenes he had never witnessed before. They would wave back at him whenever he raised his hand from the van. And every instance he would lose his balance and roll over on his bum, it would invite a roar of laughter from those ogling at his journey.

Horen enthusiastically described the neighbourhoods they crossed along the way. Every turn they took had a landmark – one crooked banyan tree, an old dry well, a single standing wall of a burnt house. And Horen had a unique story to tell for each and every one of them.

Like all the people in Polashdanga had one or more relatives who lived in Deogarh in Bihar, and almost all of them have the same surname – Mandal. Their forefathers had migrated during the great famine of 1948, and they brought with them the essence of their culture and craftsmanship. They were potters by profession, and their descendants have continued the practice. The entire village lived like one big family.

Then came Nishantola. The place had derived its name from a saffron banner hoisted atop the temple of Siddheshwar, as a symbol of hope during the dark ages of Bengal under Sultan Sulaiman Khan Karrani, whose army ravaged through the region during the sixteenth century destroying almost every symbol of Hindu religion.

Hasanchawk, on the other hand, was home to a Muslim seer who was supposedly of Portuguese descent. He was found abandoned and alone along the shores of the bay by a fakir. His entire family had been killed by pirates, and he was the lone survivor in the carnage. He got refuge in the *dargah* and embraced a new faith and a new life.

Similarly, Chhokkapukur was so called because it had six water bodies that were believed to be connected by an underground tunnel as they always had the same level of water. Chhatimpur was centred around a century-old tree that had been thrice hit by lightning and Kusumdihi was haunted by the soul of a young bride who was burnt alive with her dead husband as per the norms of the time.

The stories seemed never-ending, and so seemed the journey. Horen kept pushing hard at the paddle. But suddenly, Nando noticed a sense of alarm in his actions. It was probably due to the weather, which had undergone a rapid and drastic change right in front of their eyes. The wind had picked up pace and felt heavy, while the sky got cloaked in dark clouds that flew in from nowhere. It soon became obvious that being outdoors under the open sky was no longer advisable. Nando couldn't find any merit in the idea that they continue with their delivery routine in spite of this situation, but Horen seemed adamant. He said the stuff he couriered was of great importance to the people, and it was vital that he collects and delivers them on time. However, it seemed that Mother Nature had taken it upon herself to challenge his commitment today. The sky now looked as if it was smeared in ash, and the sun had long gone into hiding. The trees started to bow in respect of the mighty power of the wind on display. The birds were forced to take flight at a time when they usually return to their nests. Their departing entourage formed indistinct patterns across the horizon. Amidst all this chaos, the kids continued with their fun, running, and playing around the open fields, with their mothers now chasing them to take them back home. The women were having a visibly hard time, running hitherto to ensure the safety of their family and, at the same time, attending to the chores they had laid out in the open. The wind continued to grow stronger with every passing minute. With nothing substantial blocking its way, it started to wreak havoc. It was getting increasingly obvious that this was something way more powerful than a gush of unruly air. The temperature dropped drastically within a span of a few seconds. A whirlwind of leaves and dust made it hard to keep the eyes open, and the cacophony of everything combined started to deafen the ears. Even heavier things like the plough and cart could be seen dwindling while people struggled to keep their feet on the ground. And then, the sky thundered so loud that it seemed it was going to split wide open.

* * * * *

Nando sprinted across the courtyard to reach the cattle shed just in time as the rain started pouring in large cold drops. He felt thankful that wisely enough, he had decided to ditch the comfort of a pair of casual slippers while leaving home in the morning. Instead, he chose to wear his sports shoes and, had it not been for them, he would be lying flat on his face in the mud somewhere. He could hear Horen following close on his heels as he scooted with his backpack between his arms. This bag contained all his instruments, his project notes; his entire life's work. He couldn't afford to lose them under any circumstance. So, by the time he reached the shelter, the better part of him was drenched, trying to protect his belongings from the rain.

The fierce winds blew the rain in every direction, so the roof barely proved adequate for shelter. But it certainly was better than being in the open amidst the storm. Across the courtyard were two huts on either side of the corner. As much as Nando could make out through the downpour, they looked exactly similar to what kids draw in kindergarten. And inside, crouching together in the dim light of a lantern, he could see the silhouettes of a woman and a child. Unfazed by the rain, Horen rushed up and down the courtyard a couple of times, carrying the goods that he still had on him. And then he disappeared somewhere, leaving Nando completely on his own. The rain was incessant, and the winds continued to aid its cause. Wet, cold, and nervous, he started shivering helplessly. He hoped Horen had taken his suitcase inside the hut, but he hoped more for him to return. Nando had no clue where to go or what to do next. He didn't even know on whose premises he was standing. Suddenly, he smiled as the irony of the situation dawned upon him. This morning he didn't know who Horen was, yet as of this moment, his life depended on him. He knew only as much as Horen had mentioned over the last hour or so, and honestly, he knew he had no reason to believe anything he said. But it was way too late now, and Nando was left with no choice but to trust him and just hope that it paid off. Worried and tired, Nando resigned himself to fate and perched himself behind a haystack to get as comfortable as possible and try and relax till the rain stopped.

The next morning, the world would wake up to the news of cyclone Surma that had passed through parts of Bengal before entering Bangladesh and then further into Myanmar, where it would cause the worst havoc in decades. It didn't have a name, but it rose in the bay. And even though Bengal was spared from the full brunt of the storm, the impact and damage would be reckoned to be unprecedented in its history. However, being where he was, with limited access to information and the outside world, Nando wouldn't get to know about the official details of the magnitude of the storm or the expanse of its effects immediately. But what he witnessed with his own eyes as he sat under that thatched roof seemed like an exquisite, sheer, shameless display of the unfazed, naked beauty of Nature. Such was its impact that he soon forgot where he was or what he was up to – and kept gazing with bated breath as the sound of thunder echoed across the lands and bolts of silver lightning unfurled along the edges of the rain clouds that stretched till the horizon. Physics teaches that water is transparent and that the sky has no colour. But it would all seem to be a lie when you find yourself staring at a wall of water blocking your vision on all sides, trapped within the canvas of a pitch-dark sky. Nando had lost clue of time and space as his eyes continued to conjure the visuals of this horrifying extravaganza till, he felt a gentle nudge on his arm. It was a little boy, probably seven or eight years old, though it was hard to tell in the darkness. He was covered in a tarpaulin that hung from his head to his toe, and inside he carried a small torch in one hand and a plastic sheet in the other. First, he showed Nando how to put it on effectively to cover both him and his bag. Once it was done and they were ready to step into the rain, he asked Nando to follow him in his footsteps unless he wanted to make a mess of himself on the slippery ground. And then, like a commander in familiar terrain, the kid skilfully stepped on bricks placed at an accurate distance apart along the length of the courtyard, which Nando was sure to have missed had he been on his own. The hut was barely a few feet away, and in no time, they were inside, and it was warmer and cosy in there.

An hour and a half passed by, but it continued to pour incessantly. The wind gathered more strength, and as such, the storm showed no signs of waning off anytime soon. Nando was now sitting inside the hut, wearing a spare T-shirt that he carried in his backpack and a lungi – the latter being a generous offer from his hosts that Nando hesitantly accepted. Nando had packed for at least a month, which included casual clothes he preferred wearing at home, but he was in no mood to unpack his suitcase in this place, not yet. He noticed a total of three people in the household – a pale young woman, probably in the early thirties, and her two kids, a daughter, and a young son. The son, Bolai, was the one who had escorted Nando to the house while the girl, Parul, was inside, making room for his stay. The room was scantily lit by a couple of lanterns and devoid of any substantial item worth notice and hence appeared quite spacious. The walls were not cement and bricks, but just hardened clay, and at times it seemed feeble defence against the insane storm that raged outside. Necessary items like calendars, torches and umbrellas occupied the real estate on the walls. One corner of the room was partitioned by a bamboo fence. It served as a storeroom as well as a make-shift kitchen on days like this when cooking outside in the open was no longer possible. Horen seemed to be an insider in this family. He knew his way around the house and helped Nando feel at home. The woman had disappeared behind the bamboo partition immediately after greeting him, and thereafter Nando had only heard her voice giving instructions to the rest of the folks but hadn't seen her in person.

Nando was too tired to think. He casually lied on the mattress to rest and dozed off almost immediately. He didn't know how long he was asleep until Bolai came and woke him up for dinner. It was still the same situation outside, and it seemed it wasn't going to get better anytime soon. Parul was serving hot food on a plate before him. Nando was hungry, so he started eating without further ado. Horen joined him during the meal. It was only after they had finished eating, that the kids and their mother started their meal. This was the first time Nando got a good look at the woman. She wore a faded off-white sari, and the lack of any ornaments on her thin, frail frame oozed an emptiness that would surely catch the eye of any observer. It took him a while, but eventually, the truth dawned on him.

Horen had noticed Nando looking at her as he sat leaning against the wall outside the door. As soon as Nando looked at him, he smiled and said, "I know what you must be thinking. Bolai's father was a friend of mine, though he was much younger. He had studied till high school, and he could read and write as well. And he was a fiery soul, and that's not always a good thing. He wanted things different, and that was his curse. Someone who could have lived a happy life within his tiny world was gone too soon trying to do something big. What you see is what's left of his legacy; that's all the difference he could make – a young widow and two orphan children. I am positive you wouldn't believe me if I were to tell you that this woman, Minati, would have barely been out of college had she been in your place." He spoke nonchalantly, gazing out in the distance through the rain. Nando felt the pinch in his words. Having travelled extensively to remote places like this, he was well aware of the hostility that people from the city often faced. They are considered guests, tourists, outsiders – they can't possibly imagine that a man from the city might have business here or could live among them as one of their own, or even understand their suffering and plight. For these people, anybody, or anything to do with the city always boils down to opportunities and nothing else. He smiled sheepishly as he came and sat himself on the other side of the door. And then he suddenly realised that a response was due. "I wouldn't have guessed that" he uttered, his voice exuding genuine surprise as he spoke. "I must admit I figured her to be much older than that. Also, the fact that she has two kids, I guess, made it easy for me to assume so. I am sorry."

"It's okay. You need not be sorry, Sir," Horen spoke softly, passing a quick glance to the family now having food inside. "If there is one thing I know, it's that facts are only as relevant as the time and place – and this place here is worlds apart from yours. And the time, it can't be worse than this," he said in a dejected tone.

"Why do people keep saying that? What is it that I am missing here?" Nando asked Horen curiously.

Horen looked at him for a while, with calm, piercing eyes trying to assess if this boy was worth the effort to share what he knew. A few moments passed, and after a few long puffs of the hookah, he finally asked Nando, "tell me, Sir. What do you know about the Jolpaitala incident?"

⁕ ⁕ ⁕ ⁕ ⁕

The **Detour**

Nando hadn't slept so well in years, and maybe never again will, like he did that night. It was cold and quiet after the storm had passed, and everything around him seemed to be at absolute peace. Horen had snored all night laying at the corner of the room, but that didn't bother Nando a bit, who slept like a log bundled up in a blanket upon the charpoy. And in the morning, he opened his eyes with no interference by alarm clocks or honking cars – a million-dollar feeling in itself. Thankfully, this household had a closed-door sanitation facility, albeit secluded in the outdoors and without a roof. But still it was enough for Nando to not regret waking up after daybreak. Bolai was back in his element this morning. Like a little devil he was running, jumping, and screaming along the entire stretch of the place. It took Nando a little coaxing and a bar of chocolate to persuade him for a tour around the village. Nando knew he had nothing better to do, since he already knew that the road leading outside the village had been blocked by a big old tree which had been uprooted in the thunderstorm. Horen had left with the other men of the village to check the damage, but it was highly unlikely that they could clear the road soon enough for them to leave.

"Don't you go to school, Bolai?" Nando asked the boy as they began their stroll as per arrangement.

"We don't have a school here, dada. The only one nearby is in Damanpur, where you are going. And that too is closed now. Horen kaka says something big and important is going on there, and it's necessary, but I doubt it." Bolai exclaimed while waving a stick as if it were a wand or a sword.

Nando looked at him in surprise; he didn't expect to hear such a mature comment from a little boy, but Bolai remained indifferent and continued with his casual rant, "they say there are people, rich people, who are taking our lands from us. They are giving us money, but we won't be able to grow rice anymore, and we will have to work in factories. They promised we will get new houses. But some others said we won't be able to stay here anymore and that's why they refused to give up their land. They are fighting. Some are dying too, like my father, but I still don't know who is winning."

Nando kept mum and continued walking. He didn't what would be the right thing to say. Bolai then stopped and looked at him with a wry face and said, "But you know what's funny? These are the exact same things Baba wanted for me; he used to tell me that I should study and go to the city and get a job and a house. Funny, isn't it?" Bolai fell silent after saying these words, without caring for an answer.

"Did Horen tell you all this?" Nando spoke to break the uneasy quiet.

"No, of course not!" he rejected the theory outright and then uttered with a giggle "I eves-dropped when he was talking to others." Nando laughed out loud at his cute confession, and the air lightened a bit. Till then, Nando hadn't been able to muster the courage to look into the boy's sad eyes.

The night before, when they spoke, Nando had come to know from Horen about the details of the infamous Jolpaitala incident, which had made the headlines a few months back. And it went on for a few months. People were slaughtered, allegations were made, and commissions were appointed. Panel discussions and candle marches happened every second day. And then it subsided to the bottom of the information chain like all news does, and since then had only been heard in references and debates. What remained were some broken dreams and incomplete promises, which, however, never made it to the columns of the dailies.

Like most people in his city, Nando knew only as much as he had seen in news bulletins or read in print media. It all started two years ago when the incumbent government rode back to power based on an incomplete mandate. Driven by the urge to prove their mettle, they identified a hundred acres of farmland in the region as a prospective site for setting up a factory. The company that proposed to buy the land was the famous ByeBye Tire Company; the conglomerate that owned the company had signed a memorandum with the government to invest a hundred million dollars in the state over the next five years, and this was one of their pilot projects. The owners of the lands were offered a handsome amount in exchange for their land. Most agreed, some didn't. But the latter were in the minority. So, as time passed, their opposition weakened and eventually, they agreed to settle for a better offer. But the worst affected were the farmers whose livelihood depended on those lands and who remained out of the equation and were completely ignored. Yes, the ground reality was that in many instances, the landowners were an entirely separate entity than the people who worked on them; the actual farmers and peasants hardly owned any lands, and even if they did, it would mainly be mortgaged to the money-lenders. And the people who actually owned the acres had it loaned out to farmers for sharecropping on a seasonal basis while they diversified to other businesses. So, when the deal was struck, it was these people who had no option but to oppose. Initially, it was thought that the issue would not escalate and that the stakeholders would be able to settle the dispute internally. The landowners tried all means, leaving no stone unturned to silence the rebel voices. When none of that worked, the authorities stepped in. They tried to contain the opposition with force. People went missing, never to be found. Women and children were hustled, houses were vandalised. At first, goons were employed to perform the dirty job covertly; then, even the government machinery got involved. Police started arresting people on false charges and turned a deaf ear to the other side of the story. They thought it was just a matter of time before the people's strength gave way to their fears, but they were wrong. They grossly underestimated the grit of a hungry man. The tactics backfired, and the issue became political. The opposition parties grabbed the opportunity with both hands. They formed an alliance and openly came in support of the farmers. The incident ballooned into a national issue and started getting mentions in the parliament and along the corridors of the South Block. The opposition alliance also decided that the situation demanded more than just their passive and moral support. And so, the one-act play of tyranny now escalated to full-fledged guerrilla warfare. Things became worse as nobody was ready to back down. When all hope to reach a solution had died, finally, the corporation themselves entered the arena. They involved their top executives who tried to broker a deal. Where force failed, consolation did the trick. They sold the idea of employment to those farmers, a fixed income, and a better life for their children. They sold hope in exchange for their submission. The farmer unity was broken; most of them agreed to join the workforce. The few who still stood their ground were given back their lands. But it was not the same land that was taken from them. The construction work had already commenced on the grounds – the cement and mortar had taken its toll on the soil, and it was no longer the fertile land that bore rich fruit round the year. Once where rich green fields of grain bloomed, barren lands lay waste now.

But that was not the end of it. At the same time, the government had earmarked a similar project in neighbouring Damanpur – an international chemical plant in collaboration with the international Salman group of companies. After the hiatus at Jolpaitala and the complete loss of face, this time, the administration was adamant about ensuring that this project went ahead as planned. They were convinced that just like their regime, this initiative too was supposed to be of the people, for the people and by the people – even if the people themselves were too short-sighted not to understand it. They were ready to deal with this like a parent would discipline a naughty child. They were prepared to crack the whip this time.

"You know you must be really foolish to go there around this time." Bolai invaded Nando's stream of thoughts with an abrupt comment. Nando looked at him; he seemed genuinely amused at the thought.

"And why do you think so, may I ask, your honour?" Nando teased the little boy as the latter continued to fiddle with the stick in his hand, waving it hitherto here and there.

"I don't know, but I have heard it's not a good place to go anymore. People who go are not the same when they come back. And many never come back at all, like my father never came back from Jolpaitala." Nando had stopped as the boy muttered the words.

"How old are you, Bolai?" Nando asked as it took a while for the words to sink in completely.

"Mother says I will be seven this winter," he exclaimed casually. Nando was surprised. But as he scanned the boy's frail anatomy closely, it became obvious he was telling the truth. The signs of malnutrition lay etched on his skin, on his bones that protruded through his dark tan, but his skeletal structure bore testimony of his age.

They roamed around the village, witnessing the wreck left behind by the storm. People were trying to salvage the remnants of the calamity and get everything back to normal. The sky was clear, and the sun was up, but signs of the catastrophe remained littered around the roads and alleys. The rice fields were flooded; it was obvious even for a layman like Nando that a significant portion of the crops have been damaged. Not many houses had all four walls standing, as the trees that had provided them shade and shelter for years had hammered their way through them as they fell. A local tea stall, which surprisingly survived the carnage, had a radio playing, and people flocked around the device to hear the news. Nando listened anxiously as the newsreader announced in an indifferent baritone that the cyclone had hit the east coast and had caused immense destruction in various districts across the state as well the neighbouring ones. He continued to read out numbers – for casualties, damages and losses and also mentioned that the numbers were based on very simplistic assumptions and the true magnitude of the disaster, and the official estimates would only be available once the rescue teams managed to reach the worst-affected areas. Nando had no taste left for that sort of information as he stood in the middle of it all, and so he kept walking.

They came back around afternoon. Horen had already returned a while ago and was waiting for Nando. Minati was busy in the kitchen, trying to fix a lunch for all. Nando was feeling embarrassed to impose upon them during this trying times. He wanted to offer some money to Minati, for the trouble he had put them through, but somehow, he felt that it might insult their generosity and she would definitely refuse it. So, he took the easy way out by giving it as a gift to Bolai, which he knew would eventually land up where he intended to. And that's exactly what happened. Bolai handed over the money to Minati and took off as soon they reached. Parul was busy cleaning up the mess in the courtyard. Nando went and sat with Horen on the porch, overlooking the road, as they waited patiently for the food to be prepared, and that presented him with a viable opportunity to initiate a conversation.

"So, how long do you think it's going to take before the roads are cleared?" Nando started by asking the most important question he had.

"They won't be. In fact, the villagers are vying to use this situation to their benefit; with the roads blocked from this way, they are digging a trench deep enough so that nobody can enter Damanpur from the other side as well," he answered indifferently.

Nando was aghast. "Do you mean to say there is no way I can get there? After facing all this trouble and coming all this way, I have to go back empty-handed? Is that what you are saying?" he muttered as if to himself.

"Of course not, Sir. Horen is a man of his word. I will make sure you reach where you started for. And as long as you are with me, no harm will come your way, but tell me, Sir," his voice sounding an eerie sense of purpose for the first time as he turned towards Nando and looked into his eyes, "Now that you know all of it – what's been, what is and what might be, would you still want to go there? People are dying there every day. Law has lost grip, and people have lost hope. Damanpur is all but doomed. Given the circumstances, I would suggest you rather not, but...you are already here."

* * * * *

"I would suggest you rather not, but…"

Nando could vouch that these exact same words had echoed from the darkest corners of his subconscious mind a million times before. They have been haunting him for years; only the voice would differ sometimes. Nando belonged to a lineage that had been omnipresent in the administrative circles of Bengal for many decades. His family's influence dated back to the pre-independence era. His grandfather had worked in the Bengal provincial police force and went on to retire as the DIG of Bengal Police in independent India. His brother graduated from JNU and went on to work for the Indian Foreign Services. Nando's father occupied a senior post at the Board of Education in West Bengal. His elder sister, was a hugely reputed cardiac surgeon who chaired numerous government councils. So, coming from this family, it was only expected of Nando to be the absolute best and claim his place among the few at the top. And he tried. He put his best effort to excel at everything they wanted for him to be. But sometimes, even his best wasn't good enough. And for that, he was looked down upon in his own family, among his kin, even by his own father. He wouldn't say anything directly to Nando, but even as a kid, he could see the utter disdain in his father's eyes whenever his son's name came up in a discussion. He could feel he was the one who got labelled as the black sheep of the family. One time he even overheard his father cracking a joke about how he owed his lesser skills to his mother's side. Nando's mother came from a relatively humble background – she wasn't as highly educated as her in-laws, and neither had anybody in her family accomplished much to brag about. But they were nice people, and Nando somehow felt more comfortable in their company than at his own house. His mother was a homemaker, and she was exceptional at it. She never gave anybody any chance to complain, yet she had to face a fair share of criticism because of Nando's failures. She was soft-spoken by nature and seldom participated or reacted to banter. She loved reading and had got Nando into the same habit at an early age. And so, every time he felt sad or upset, Nando found refuge and solace behind the covers of a book.

Nando managed to score a decent enough percentage in his board exams. While that wasn't good enough to get him into medical school, which his father would have liked, he still had enough to get him into an engineering college or a law school. But Nando knew that was not what he wanted – he had a genuine inclination towards biology and was especially keen to study about plants and soil. This was a dream only he knew about, and no one else did. That is no one else in his family. Because there was one more person who knew about it and, as a matter of fact, had been quite a defining force behind this dream. That person was Surjo.

Nando met him during one of his summer visits to his maternal uncle's place on vacation when he was in high school. His father was away as a part of an official delegation to parts of Europe and America at that time. So, his mother managed to pay a rare and welcome visit to her native place. They lived in a small little town along the uplands of Bihar, surrounded by lush green mountains and sparsely populated hamlets and villages. The area offered an entire spectrum when it came to the soil textures and the kind of vegetation that grew on them. His uncle introduced him to a local lad to show him around, who used to conduct field trips for the local schools. Surjo was that guy. The first time Nando met him, he formed an instant liking for this tall, dark, lanky fellow who stood on the porch scratching the mud with a rock and making designs. He was quite a few years elder to Nando, and given the extensive time he spent outdoors, he carried a rather ruffian look. He had dropped out of school for reasons best known to him. His parents were business folks, people who lacked formal education but possessed significant wealth, and they allowed their son all the freedom to follow his own will.

So, he would happily spend his time with the local villagers and even visit the remote corners of the forest that covered the hills to rendezvous with the natives. He tried to learn all sorts of wild, weird stuff from them – hunting, exorcism and similar things that were looked down upon by civil society. Sometimes he would be gone for months, travelling with the gypsies to odd and remote places. Initially, his parents would get worried sick and deploy every resource at their disposal to find him, but that almost never worked. And then, one fine day, he would come back on his own, telling tall tales of fascinating experiences. No one could vouch for the authenticity of these stories, but they did reflect his profound knowledge on some earthly matters. They would usually contain very vivid descriptions of the places he claimed to have been to – he would describe the people, landscapes, the flora, and fauna so well that even a stranger would be able to visualise it distinctly. He would claim to have performed heroic exploits, and that gathered him quite a fan following over a period of time, especially among the kids. He seemed to know it all – which river flowed in which valley, which plant grew best in which soil, and how much it usually rained in some remote village in the jungle. So, it was no surprise that Nando, too, was attracted to his antics just like many others of his age. And indeed, that trip proved to be the best two weeks of his life. They bonded immediately, probably because they both had very little knowledge of the other's world. Surjo had never been to Kolkata, and he had as many questions about the city as Nando had about the wilderness. During one of these conversations, in order to impress Surjo, Nando showed him one of his most precious possessions – a Chinese video game console.

It was a very basic hand-held device. It came in all the tacky, loud colours that could attract young minds, probably to camouflage the fact it looked a bit like their pencil boxes. And the games were basic too – like laying bricks and building blocks quicker than usual or an obstacle run by a tiny insect-sized character. But these were a rage during those times, as they were the first of their kind. Almost every kid had one, and those who didn't, made their parent's lives miserable by constantly nagging for one.

Surjo held it like a piece of jewellery as he ogled at it for a few good seconds. He seemed to be mesmerised by it.

"You get to play with such wonderful toys?" he finally asked when he managed to get a hold of his emotions.

"That's all we get to play with," Nando had responded, visibly dampening the excitement that shone in Surjo's eyes a moment ago.

There's something magical about adolescence, where bonds are made with mere words.

"You can keep it if you like it." Nando had offered generously.

"I will think about it if you promise to meet me here tonight. I think I might have a gift for you as well. Sneak out quietly when everybody has slept," Surjo had said while handing him back his gadget.

"I can't leave like that, quietly, without telling anyone. What if somebody finds out? They will punish me. They might even bar me from talking to you ever again," Nando had mentioned nervously.

Surjo had put a hand on his shoulder, like one brother to another, and said with a smile, "Then you will never know what you can have, besides what they have given you." And then he had left.

The words left a lasting impression on Nando's young mind. But he still wasn't convinced. The fear of reprimand was too big. But then, as night approached and everybody retired to their own sweet comfort zones, a voice started whispering in Nando's mind. A voice that sounded a lot like his. A voice that wouldn't stop until he decided to get up and step out.

The night was cold and wintry. The sky was empty, except for a crescent moon that barely illuminated the earth. Nando waited patiently at the designated point as the minutes seemed never-ending. He could literally hear his heart beat; there were a million things that went through his mind, and most of them were alarmingly scary thoughts. He can't remember how long he had to wait, but he can vouch every moment of that period he was battling the thought of turning back. In fact, he still wasn't sure what made him stay – what was it that made him so desperate. He didn't even know if he could trust the boy he had barely known for a week. But he felt he could.

He wasn't wrong. Surjo didn't ditch him that night. He came late and seemed absolutely ignorant to that fact. They didn't exchange any words. He quietly signalled Nando to follow as he got off the trodden path and into the fields. And he seemed to know his way even in the middle of that barren, listless stretch of land. Nando was having trouble even figuring out his left from his right in that place when he looked around in that emptiness. He was too young to understand it then, that what seemed an aimless void to him was almost home to his companion.

After a few minutes of a walk leading them away from the last of house to be seen, they finally arrived where Surjo intended. He didn't have to say it out loud. Nando knew it when he saw it. It was like all the stars in the sky had come to visit what lay beneath them. The place was dark and moist and almost completely covered in large trees whose roots run deep. Their branches created canopies that blocked the view above, and the ground was littered with dead leaves and mud. And sprinkled among that stinky filth were these tiny twinkling lights. They weren't fireflies; these lights were way more static, like bright, little polka dots on a dark, blue curtain hiding the sky. A closer look might have revealed their reality, but from a distance and that place and time, they seemed magical to the two teenagers. It wasn't just beautiful or breath-taking. It was beyond belief.

Surjo would gleefully accept the game console as a gift the next morning. Nando would never again ask for another one and, instead, read whatever he could lay his hands upon until he learned about the springtails that were responsible for making those magical lights. He would eventually lose touch with Surjo but would never forget him. He would grow up to be a bookworm with immense interest in the study of biological sciences.

While his father was impressed at this development, assuming his son aspired to be a doctor one day, his mother knew the real fact. Nando would spend all his pocket money to buy geographic magazines and journals, and when he fell short, he would reach out to her. While she never denied her son his slice of happiness, she always remained wary of the fact that his father would never approve of the plans that brewed in his mind.

She was right to be worried. Nando was fascinated with a very specific study that dealt with earth's geology and climate. This subject held the key to the door that would lead him back to the world where trees and soil glow in the dark. However, this was definitely not among the more lucrative career options in the country. The minimal opportunities of work would give nightmares to any concerned parent. And in Nando's case, his mother feared it would cause mayhem if his father and the rest of his family got to know about his intentions. And precisely, that is what happened.

At the first opportunity he got, Nando applied to the Indian Institute of Soil Sciences in Bhopal to work as an intern. When the information leaked to the family, all hell broke loose. His relatives spoke to other relatives, made rude comments and comparisons. Unwarranted advice started pouring in. And the one person who mattered the most, his father, completely shut himself off. He stopped talking to Nando altogether. It seemed as if he no longer featured in his list of priorities. It was almost as if his younger son had ceased to exist for him. Of course, he remained aware of all of Nando's endeavours from his mother, and he even agreed to pay for his "whim" as he considered it to be. But he wouldn't even talk to him about it or try to counsel or dissuade him. And that made Nando all the more adamant and coaxed him to pursue his passion with renewed vigour. There was just one time this barrier was broken. It was when Nando approached him for the mandatory signature of a parent. There was a moment when Nando felt that there lived a concerned father somewhere beneath the shell and that his eyes echoed the pain his son was causing him by being stubborn. Nando wanted to sit down with him, talk to him, and share his dreams with him. But all his father said was, "I would suggest you rather not, but...I guess you will anyway." And that's how that conversation ended even before it began.

* * * * *

The **Arrival**

The journey to Damanpur was an arduous one, and the only reason Nando could make it was because he travelled with Horen, who seemed to know every nook and crevice of the place like the back of his palm. The manner in which he guided him through a terrain that was completely uncharted and mostly unfit for travel left no scope for doubt. The marks left behind by the storm could be seen everywhere. But even then, one could sense that there was something else going on besides the standard relief and rescue work by the locals. And it was the same scenario on the school premises as well, where Nando was meant to meet Surjo. Nando had got back in touch with him a few months back for his own selfish interests. He needed Surjo's help for a very important project. Unfortunately, his planning and preparations took more time than he thought it would, and so he ended up here a few months later than when he would have wanted to.

The schoolhouse at Damanpur was a simple structure — it had two floors and was painted in white and blue.

It overlooked a small square compound, enveloped between a park and a pond on either side. Upon a quick glance, it would not seem much with its pale, damp walls, a few broken windows, and the damaged wooden doors, but it was obviously the very best they could have done. The structure ensured the best utilization of the space available and accommodated the maximum number of rooms possible. On any other day, one would see hundreds of children flocking in and out of the building. And when the classes started, one could hear the sound of chalk rubbing against the blackboards. But not today. Today, the place looked like a warzone.

Fliers and festoons crisscrossed the entire width of the place, creating an overhead mesh. If one happened to look up at the sky, they might feel they are looking at it through a cage. Scores of people scampered around, fixing things that needed attention. Makeshift counters had been constructed to serve as offices. One of them had a microphone that was being used to make important announcements. Funnel-shaped speakers were mounted on trees, and Nando could hear them from a mile away. Horen had disappeared inside the building the moment they reached, leaving Nando stranded in the company of some local young guys. They were occupied with painting ensigns and discussing politics as best they knew. But the presence of an outsider was not lost on them, and they kept on passing sceptic glances at him. Nando tried to start a conversation, beginning with an awkward smile. But when that failed to generate even a lukewarm response, he decided it was best to avoid their company and check out the posters till someone came to fetch him. He walked up to the shade where the placards and banners have been stacked. The makers had used red and black paint to scribble things on them, mostly phrases and slogans that spoke about peasants and farmers – their plights and their purpose, their rights, and their rebellion. Nando had never considered himself any good at affairs and agendas of the civil society. He believed all a person can do is be the best version of himself, and that itself should make the world a better place over a generation or two. He believed that attempts to influence someone else's thoughts and actions almost always led to trouble and seldom yielded results. He was also convinced that looking out for a fellow human being is a virtue best practised only when one's own priorities are sorted. However, everybody in Damanpur seemed to believe otherwise. All the people present there seemed genuinely concerned about the morality of people and their practices. They were convinced that the world needed correction and that responsibility fell upon anyone who could see the faults and willing to act on it. Once again, Nando felt completely out of place but in a manner entirely different than what he had expected.

He loitered around a bit until he noticed a big, old oak tree near the fence. He decided to sit under its shade while he waited. But before he could do so, a warning voice sounded from behind, "be careful! the ground is still wet over there." Nando quickly turned around to find a lanky, pale fellow smiling at him. Nando now checked the ground beneath him carefully and realized he was speaking the truth. He smiled back at the person and said, "thanks for that, mister. I hadn't noticed. But honestly, I don't mind a little mud. Most of my work usually involves a lot of it." The man nodded his head slightly and left. However, a couple of other folks eyed him suspiciously as they walked by. They were probably surprised at the sight of an unknown young man from the city in the middle of all this. Nando ignored their attention as he felt happy at just being noticed. This gesture could well serve as the icebreaker, he thought. He looked around and found a wet log lying on the ground a couple of feet away and sat himself down on it. And then he took out a bundle of notes from his backpack and casually started to flip through the pages. If all went well, he told himself, the contents of these pages could take him places. "Touch wood," he whispered as he gently touched the log he was sitting on.

A few minutes passed by before Nando noticed Horen walking towards him. He was accompanied by a few other people. The man leading the pack was a tall, dark, bearded fellow. He looked like a completely different man than what Nando remembered, but he still brought a smile on his face. He quickly stood up, dusted the back of his pants, as the person walked up to him and hugged him tightly while the others waited behind. "It's so nice to see you, mate, after such a long time." Surjo's voice echoed genuine warmth as he embraced his friend.

"You have grown some muscles," Nando quipped cheekily as Surjo let go of him a few seconds later. "And you seem to have grown a brain, and maybe a couple of balls too," Surjo responded as they both broke into laughter.

"I must admit it took me a while to recognise you. You have changed so much," Nando mentioned as they started walking towards the building. The others followed them at a distance.

"I hope you mean changed for good, right?" Surjo asked with a broad smile on his face as he put his arm around Nando.

"So, tell me, how have you been, and what have you been up to? How are things back home?" Surjo continued to shoot his questions impatiently.

"I am good, and so is everybody back home. And as for what I do, I think you already know that from my letter. In fact, that is why I am here. And as I have already mentioned, I can't do this without your help," Nando replied earnestly as he adjusted his backpack over his shoulders.

"Yes, your letter, of course. Don't worry. I will help you. I think what you are doing is great, and necessary, much like what we are trying to do here," Surjo said in an unusually sombre tone, and his entire demeanour changed for a second. Nando was a bit flustered at this sudden transformation, and Surjo noticed that. He immediately lightened the air as he added with a smile, "but once you are done with yours, ours might get a bit easier."

"I hope there won't be a problem?" Nando asked nervously.

Surjo gauged the situation as soon as he heard Nando's voice. "You mean, apart from all this?" Surjo cajoled, still sporting a wry smile on his face. An awkward moment of silence followed as Surjo quietly glanced at everything going on around him. Then he turned to face Nando, who now looked visibly concerned and overwhelmed.

"Now don't you get all nervous, buddy," Surjo uttered aloud as he managed to pull up a huge grin on his face. He gently nudged Nando's rib cage with his elbow. "You are still the same, huh! I guess I was wrong about your balls after all." He pulled Nando closer and slapped his back to cheer him up. That helped bring a smile back to Nando's grim face.

Surjo took him around the place and introduced him to the young men and women Nando had seen earlier. Rathin, Mandar, Sajjad, Arunima, and a few others whose names Nando failed to register in one go. They all turned out to be university students with a firm ideological affiliation as well as genuine social concern. Of course, they were here upon instructions from their respective political leaderships, but they all seemed completely committed to the cause. Among them was a stubby, dark girl, overseeing all the activities and passing instructions wherever needed. She was undoubtedly very young, but her confidence and attitude commanded respect.

"That's Sumitra, one of our youngest and most resilient cadres. She is in charge of our entire public awareness campaign and has almost single-handedly ensured that people across the state know what we are doing here. And she is just in the first year of college. Trust me when I tell you, this girl has it in her to lead a thousand men and rewrite the course of history if she puts her mind to it," Surjo uttered in a proud voice as he introduced the two of them. She greeted him with a typical *Namaskar*. Nando was still not quite comfortable with this form of greeting; he was more used to a handshake. But to Sumitra, it came organically, as was evident in her poise and presentation.

Horen's detailed briefing of the ongoing crisis was proving helpful to Nando, as he felt he could now relate to the emotions of those he met and maybe understand the rationale behind their activities and arrangements. Surjo, too, was relieved to know that Nando knew what was going on; it made his situation a little easier.

As they sat over a cup of tea in one of the empty classrooms, Surjo started explaining to Nando "as you can see, this was a school – it has ceased to become what it is supposed to be and now serves as a centre for people's rebellion. I know this is not a good thing, but it is necessary. I don't expect you to agree or understand, and neither do I want you to get involved. It might be hard for you to believe it at this moment, but trust me when I tell you, things might turn ugly anytime. We all know that, and we have prepared for that as well. But it all happened so soon that I didn't get a chance to warn you about it. But now that you are here, it's my duty to keep you away from harm's way. And as I said, I will do as much as I can to make sure your purpose here is fulfilled. But you have to promise me something – that you will follow every instruction given to you, no questions asked, and won't try to get involved in anything that does not concern your work. If you agree to these terms, only then will I allow you to stay. Otherwise, you are leaving right now."

* * * * *

The schoolhouse being occupied, and the village being practically under siege with barricades and blockades, Surjo had to arrange Nando's accommodation in a big, old house in the outskirts. It was a thirty-minute walk and Surjo gave him clear directions to the place. But it would have been a long and lonely walk for Nando had it not been for the lanky fellow he had met in the compound earlier. He offered to give him company as well as guide him along the way. Nando found him to be a rather nice chap, a little less serious than the others he had met until then. His name was Fatik, a local lad almost the same age as Nando. He said he stayed in the same direction where Nando was headed, so he tagged along. And he kept on describing the places they crossed, just like Horen. It was fascinating for Nando to realize how proudly they related to everything about this ordinary place.

He left Nando at the gates of what looked more like a mansion than a house. It overlooked the river to which the road led and was fenced at the far end by the canal, which literally was a floating mass of green at present. It was almost impossible to access the property from either of those sides without being spotted. It was obvious to Nando that the makers had put a lot of thought into its security when the building was designed.

A single look at the architecture was enough to reveal that it was more than a hundred years old. The better part of it was now in ruins, apart from few row houses at the front, which obviously had been built more recently. It was in one of them that Nando found Mr. Ghosal.

Mr. Pramod Ghosal was an old man for sure, though Nando couldn't really figure out if he was in his late fifties or early seventies. Some people grow old with age, with time, and then there are some who grow old by virtue of what they have seen and done in whatever time they have lived. It becomes really tough to count their age in years anymore. Mr. Ghosal surely belonged to this second group. He was the one in charge of looking after this property, as its current ownership was still being disputed in court. He showed Nando around while talking about its history.

"The village derives its name, Damanpur, from the first owner of this house, Mr. Damien Wiltshire. He was an Englishman who had served in the Royal British army for many years. It is said that he had been to remote lands and fought many wars before he came to India. Once he arrived here, however, things changed. Some say he fell in love with this place. Others say he was lured by the wealth he saw around. But whatever may be the reason, he decided to stay, and he bought lands and built this house with the wealth he had accumulated over his years of service."

Mr. Ghosal narrated the story as they went around the building, and Nando could literally feel the grandeur that it once represented. The main building had two floors, but it was high enough to tower over the coconut trees that stood in its backyard. It stood on the right as one entered through the gate, overlooking the river at the far left. The ground floor had an open corridor stretching to the far end, and the doors lining its length faced the open courtyard. The stairs leading to the first floor were right in the middle of the corridor. The first floor had the same layout, with the exception of arches and rails between pillars covering the balcony. But the noticeable difference was that the far side of the floor was closed with a concrete wall. It blocked the corridor as well as the balcony, rendering that part of the building completely out of reach. The walls however had little windows along its length below the arches. It was as if they wanted to hide what's in there but let it have a peek outside. Nando, however, didn't bother asking that to Mr. Ghosal, as there were too many thoughts going through him mind as they wandered around the property. The lack of care was getting evident as they slowly moved inside. The rear end of the property was in complete ruins. Most of it had reclaimed by nature, with small green leaves sprouting from every nook and corner of the broken walls and pillars. The floor above was literally in shambles there, after been wrecked in a devastating fire a few decades ago. Anyone wandering into that part unaware was sure to face a horrible death. Maybe that's why they had shut it with a wall, Nando thought. It was obvious that the wall was erected recently, as it bore a stark contrast to the rest of the architecture.

"The original idea was to separate the disputed part, of course. We call it the solitary wall," Mr. Ghosal mentioned proactively, and then went on to add "I think the storm has damaged a part of it." Once they were done with the tour, they came and sat in one of the row houses which served as an office for the public welfare association of which Mr. Ghosal was the appointed chief. There were three of them, built across the courtyard, halfway through its length. They also served the purpose of hiding the ruins from any onlooker. The one on the left served as a library for the people while the third one served as clinic. They all operated between ten to five on weekdays.

Nando couldn't help skimming through the books as they entered the library. He was genuinely fond of books and could pick one up anytime, anywhere. The collection wasn't that big; they merely had few hundred, but the variety was impressive. It contained a bit of everything from traditional European classics to contemporary

Indian literature – a gold mine spanning centuries and eras. As Nando stood engrossed, flipping through the pages of an ancient copy of Don Quixote, Mr. Ghosal had walked up to him unnoticed.

"It seems you have a taste for good literature," he quipped with a smile as he watched Nando checking the books with genuine interest.

Nando looked up and smiled. "I must admit this collection has significantly outdone my expectations. Any top institution across the globe would be proud to have such a collection."

"Then let me add to your surprise, mister. This is not even a quarter of what we had in our original collection. There was a brilliant library in that part of the building. The collection we have in here is nothing compared to what remains locked up in there. It's a shame." he uttered as he led Nando outside and into the main building.

As they made their way up the stairs, Mr. Ghosal mentioned that there was only one single room on the first floor, to the left of the stairs, which had been renovated to make it fit for living for a short duration. The area to the right was blocked by the wall, and a pile of junk that remained stacked against it. But even from a distance it was obvious, that just like the rest of the village, the storm had caused some damage to the wall as well.

Nando looked at it and then looked at Mr. Ghosal, who simply gave a sad, wry smile and made his way towards the room. "It might not be much, but you could indulge in the fact that once the lords lived here," Mr. Ghosal cajoled as he opened the door. It was a big room with a simple setup, containing a cupboard, a chair and a table with an earthen pot mounted on it to store drinking water. And planted right in the middle of the room, was a huge bed made of teakwood and sporting intricate designs reminiscent of imperial India.

Mr. Ghosal had got hold of a local lad to help Nando with his everyday chores. He was a young fellow in his early teens and was visibly a little dumb. Everybody in the village fondly called him *Boka Bishu*, but they all loved him for his honesty and hard work. He quickly cleaned the room, fetched enough drinking water to last Nando the night, and then got them some tea from a shop across the alley. It was almost sundown, and Mr. Ghosal was about to leave. Nando still had the food that Minati had packed him before they started, so he was good. Mr. Ghosal briefed Bishu to come back the next morning, and then as he prepared to leave, he turned to Nando and said, "Unfortunate as it is, I must advise caution given the situations around here and more so because you are a stranger to these places. If I were you, I would avoid stepping out of the room at night unless absolutely required. And remember, nights begin early around here, and it gets pretty dark. Stay indoors, and you will be alright." He stressed on every word he uttered and then after wishing him a good night, he left.

Nando anyway had no intentions to wander off anywhere in the night. He had never felt so tired in his whole like he did after making that three-hour-long journey to Damanpur. He was dying to dive into the bed and go to sleep as soon as possible. Bishu was still lingering around in case Nando needed any assistance. He had already gotten two buckets of water from the well and kept it in the washroom as there was no running water supply on the first floor. He waited patiently while Nando took a shower and had his food. He wasn't hungry, and the food was cold. But he still ate a bit as he didn't want to throw the food. Bishu was sitting on the floor next to the door, grinning for no good reason. Nando took out his wallet and gave him a ten-rupee note. His joy was evident as his eyes brightened up and his smile grew wider. He kept the money carefully in his pocket, and amusing Nando out of his wits, the fool threw him a full military salute and turned back and marched away. Nando closed the door, dimmed the lantern, and lay down on the bed with a book, but even before he could turn to the first page, he dozed off.

His slumber broke sometime in the wee hours of the night. He was thirsty and cold. Thankfully, the lantern was still burning, but it was almost out of fuel. Nando checked his watch; the radium dial showed it was ten past two. Unlike the previous night when a storm raged outside his walls, it was so awfully quiet today, that one might wonder whether the living world has ceased to exist. He looked outside the window. It was pitch dark, without a simmer of light for miles ahead. Nando sat up on the bed. His book was lying face down next to him; he picked it up and kept it on the table. There was still some water left in his bottle. He gulped it down and then reached out for the earthen pot mounted on his table. The water was unpredictably cold, and it shook up his drowsy senses. And it was then that he noticed the sound – a composition of the constant chirping of crickets aptly coupled with the grunting of the frogs from the nearby marshlands, and the occasional hooting of an owl piercing the monotony. But the completely unexpected and awkward intrusion to this cacophony was a male baritone, faint yet flawless, muttering something in crisp Victorian English. It was so close and clear, that Nando even recognized the words. They were verses by John Keats –

Can death be sleep, when life is but a dream?
And scenes of bliss pass as a phantom by?
The transient pleasures as a vision seem,
And yet we think the greatest pain's to die.
How strange it is that man on earth should roam,
And lead a life of woe, but not forsake
His rugged path; nor dare he view alone
His future doom which is but to awake.

* * * * *

The **Stay**

Oblivious to the noise as the village woke up to its usual early routine, Nando slept like a log till Bishu came and knocked on the door the next morning. It was quarter past nine, quite late for the rural way of life. Nando felt a bit embarrassed as he opened the door, but Bishu seemed indifferent. As always, he was grinning away happily for no obvious reason as he held up a paper foil soaked in oil. Nando hastily freshened up as Bishu emptied the contents of the foil in a paper plate. They were freshly fried *kachori* and *alur dom*. Nando's father had always had strict regulations regarding food, and these items were not allowed in his household as there was nothing remotely healthy about them. But that didn't stop Nando from binging on these classic Kolkata delicacies every now and then. He and his friends would plan it together post their early morning swimming lessons at the lake. But even those were nothing compared to what he was having now – this smelled like a slice of heaven, and the tasted like pure bliss. Nando felt the person making this was no less than an artist. He made an animated gesture to Bishu to show how much he liked it as he continued to munch and savour every morsel he put in his mouth. Bishu's face lighted up once again upon seeing his happy face.

Bishu had also arranged for a warm cup of ginger tea to compliment the food, and that was all Nando could have asked for. As he sipped on it, leaning on the pillow on the bed, he felt that there could not be a better start to his day. All that he was missing was a newspaper. Nando had a habit of scanning through the last few pages every day to stay updated about every game of almost every sport played on this planet. And then, he would slowly make his way to the front page, only after gorging on every bit of gossip about the movie stars and their shenanigans. This helped create a perfect prelude to the political mudslinging detailed in the front pages. But being where he was on this day, Nando didn't feel the rush of missing out on any news of what was going on in the outside world. Whether Sachin was fit to play, or how Shah Rukh hurt himself on sets, or if the Prime Minister was visiting South Korea once again – none of that seemed relevant out here.

Content and happy, Nando casually strolled out to the balcony, lit a cigarette, and let off a huge puff of smoke. He had always wanted to do this. At home, whenever he felt the urge, he had to sneak up to the roof, hide behind the water tank and quickly finish the job, checking every now and then if somebody was watching. But not here.

This felt good, all of it. Lost in his thoughts, Nando didn't notice when Bishu had walked up and stood right next to him. He was grinning, as usual, making Nando wonder if he should offer him a smoke too. How old is he, he thought in his mind, and even if he is old enough, should I be offering him smoke? Diverted by his dilemma, Nando could not comprehend what Bishu had spoken in the meantime. So, he looked back at him and asked, "Did you say something?"

"No, I was just asking if you slept well last night, Dada," he quipped, with an unmistakable tinge of concern in his voice.

"As a matter of fact, I can't tell you how well I have actually slept. Barring the intrusion of a few mosquitoes, which is understandable, there was nothing else to complain about" Nando exclaimed, looking at Bishu as he did. And much to his surprise, he felt that Bishu was disappointed upon his positive response. He kept looking at Nando as if he expected to hear something more. Nando pondered for a while, and then mentioned "the only other thing I can remember is the crowing of the roosters in the neighbourhood at dawn. But there's nothing one could do about that." He chuckled at his own joke, trying to shrug off any further questions. Bishu got the hint and remained quiet. Nando continued to enjoy his cigarette, making rings in the air. And then, just like that, out of the blue, he remembered the voice – the deep baritone he thought he heard in the middle of the night. He looked at

Bishu, staring blankly for a while before he felt amused at his stupidity – he must have had a dream. He wondered what Bishu would have thought had he mentioned it and laughed out loud at the very thought. Bishu looked at him, surprised.

"What happened, Dada? Something funny you saw?" the boy asked curiously.

Nando shook his head as he continued to smile, "I just remembered a silly dream I had last night."

"You heard him, didn't you?" Bishu muttered softly as he narrowed his eyes with his gaze fixed on Nando's face.

Nando was startled. "What are you talking about?" he asked, making no attempt to hide his surprise.

"The voice," Bishu uttered shakily, eyes wide open and beads of sweat appearing on his forehead. "A dark, husky voice chanting something in a weird language. You heard it, right?"

"Not a chant. What I heard was an English poem. As far as I could remember it was Keats. But how the hell do you know about this?" Nando was shuddering at the thought of what Bishu was trying to imply. "You mean to say it wasn't a dream, and the voice was for real?" he finally managed to ask.

"I knew it, I always knew it. And now I have my proof." Bishu was ecstatic, jumping and punching in the air with his fists, completely oblivious to the shock Nando was experiencing. "They didn't believe me, but they will now. They have to." he kept repeating like a man possessed, until he noticed that Nando was not there anymore. He peeked inside the room to find Nando sitting at the edge of the bed with his head stooping down and lost in deep thoughts.

"Sorry, Dada, if I have upset you," Bishu said apologetically as he was back to his senses and took his usual place near the door. Nando turned towards him, confused and disturbed. "Please hear me out," Bishu begged.

"Go ahead," Nando replied, unable to camouflage his discomfort.

"It was a long time ago – I was maybe five or six years old. Me and my best friend, Moinul, used to hang around a lot together. He stayed a few blocks away from me. We went to the same school. And every day, we would walk back home together. We were good friends because, just like me, he, too, shied away from playing with the other kids. While I avoided physical sports because I was frail compared to others of my age, Moinul genuinely had no interest in it. He would rather spend that time wandering around the village, being happy in little things that most people don't even notice or choose to ignore. He was unique. During summer, he would visit a dry riverbed and claim to have found something special hidden below the cracks, or he would sneak into an old, abandoned garden and spend hours looking at rotting old trees, waiting for something spectacular to happen.

"I too knew someone like that when I was your age," Nando interrupted with a smile as fond memories came flooding back to him. He lit another cigarette and signalled to Bishu to continue with his story.

"Moinul would tell stories about them, and he would make them sound so interesting that soon enough, I was lured to follow him. And then I saw them too, those places and those things. And when I saw them the way he did, they did seem fascinating."

"Now, as kids, we were always asked to stay away from this mansion. This was before the municipalities took over the place and began renovation work. Back then, it was just a broken house where nobody had lived for more than a century. It anyway looked spooky enough to keep people away. Behind this building, there used to be a big open garden enclosed within its fences, that stretched all the way up to the canal. We had seen only as much was visible from the other side. Even then, it wasn't much more than a big square plot of land densely populated with trees and bushes, so much so that one could barely see through them. And everybody avoided that part as much as they avoided the house because there was more than one reason to be afraid. But Moinul had a weird idea. He said he had seen a tree among the foliage that glowed in the dark. Even by his standards, that was by far the most insane claim he had ever made. But he was completely convinced. He kept coaxing me to accompany him. I was scared and tried to dissuade him as well. But he was desperate. He lived in his own world of whims, and his passion knew no bounds in these matters. So instead, he managed to convince me."

Bishu paused at this time. Nando's eyes were fixated on him, and he could clearly see the expression of pain and angst clouding the boy's face. He quietly waited until Bishu could gather himself. But he was so invested in the story that those few moments seemed to test his patience. He felt relieved when the boy started talking again.

"I was very young, and what happened was so haunting that I can't seem to recall all the details accurately. I remember we rowed to the old quay at the back of the building, which like the rest of it, was in ruins as well. We waited till sundown on the same dinghy that had carried us there. Then we slowly crept up the stairs towards the trees that lined the bank. Moinul led the way. He seemed as confident about the location of the tree as he was about its existence. But it was a struggle to move forward through the dense population of thorny hedges and bushes. We continued moving east, and Moinul said that we would reach the tree any moment. And that's when it happened."

"First, it appeared like black smoke, a distorted lump of darkness floating and drifting in the middle of the white mist settling around us. And then it came closer, and the contours formed the shape of a human. In a while, it started looking like a tall figure in a coat, with a pale white face and blonde hair. Both of our feet froze where we stood as we laid eyes upon this abomination. Cold sweat poured from every part of us while the figure loomed around, looking right through us with its hollow eyes. I have no clue how long we stood like that. I guess we were too scared to even faint. Or at least I was. And I thought Moinul was too, till he moved. I shivered like a dry leaf in the wind as I watched him step forward. His eyes were gleaming, and his hands stretched forward – his curiosity had got the better of his fear. The look on his face; that was not the friend I knew; it was a guy searching for something extraordinary who seemed to have finally found it.

Then the figure said something, in English, I think. Neither of us understood any of it. But it was obvious that it was angry. Moinul stopped once again, as it continued to speak, indistinctly and sporadically, for a minute or two. And then, suddenly, he turned towards us and uttered the words *"Berie jao"* in a distorted, old Bengali dialect, his fingers pointing behind us. These were his first words we understood, and it meant exactly what we thought it wanted – for us to leave."

Bishu's voice choked at this point, and his eyes grew moist. Nando could see the boy was in distress. But however weird the story sounded; Nando felt compelled to learn the rest of it.

"I still can't exactly put together how the rest of it happened. We ran as soon as we heard the words. I know I did, and I pulled Moinul along. It was hard to run through the bushes. We stumbled a few times, got cuts and scratches all over. We were almost at the river when it happened. A loud searing noise erupted behind us, followed by a huge thrust that lifted us off the ground and threw us a few feet away. Last thing I remember seeing before I passed out, was Moinul's face, smeared in blood, his temple smashed open against a pile of bricks."

"He died?" an exasperated Nando asked.

"He was killed" Bishu uttered as he looked at him in the eye.

"Why are you telling me this story?" Nando asked bitterly.

"Because you are the one staying here tonight, alone and all by yourself" Bishu answered in a mellow yet sour voice, "I would suggest you rather not, but…it's too late for that now."

* * * * *

The evening was even more beautiful than the dawn. Nando was lying casually on his bed, smoking a cigarette, and gazing aimlessly at the horizon through the window. The sky was crimson with shades of purple and blue, and dotted with birds flocking back to their homes. It was a quaint and peaceful sight, and yet his mind remained occupied with the bizarre mesh of stories that surrounded him. On one side was the spooky, unreal anecdote that Bishu shared in the morning that would make no sense to any person with a sane mind. On the other hand, was this highly political issue which seemed to have so many different layers and perspectives. Nando wasn't sure he could understand any of it even if he tried really hard. And he was in the middle of it all, an eternally confused and incessantly stubborn big-city teenager trying to prove a point. It all coexisted in the same world and yet seemed worlds apart.

Lost in his thoughts, Nando didn't notice when the light of day had faded and darkness had set in. When he did, he hurriedly got up, lit the lantern on the table and stepped out on the balcony. The dim bulb outside the gates was on, and people could be heard loitering in the tea stall across the road. His eyes travelled over the rails all the way to the other end of the corridor, to the solitary wall blocking the passage beyond. His eyes remained fixed on it, as did his thoughts. And that was when he noticed it. A part of the wall, a corner to be precise, was broken. The pile of rubble dumped in front of the wall covered most of it. But one could still get a peek at the that existed on the other side. Just the imagination of the voice emanating from that hollow hole, sent a chill down Nando's spine. Bishu's creepy story that seemed like a child's imagination earlier was now proving to be very disconcerting to him.

The uncomfortable feeling stayed with him as he freshened up and made his way back to the room. He shut the door, changed into his nightclothes, and decided to go over his notes and field logs once again. He needed to know the baseline and statistics well before starting his work. But all his attempts to distract his mind proved futile. Disgusted with himself, he threw the notes and picked up another smoke. He had packed enough to last him through the trip, but he was also conscious that he was using them more frequently than he had planned for. He usually didn't indulge in more than two in a day, unless there was something seriously bothering him. But unfortunately, that seemed to be his perpetual mental state since the time he had arrived at this place. For such exceptional situations, he usually preferred something stronger – a habit he had picked up during college, and a pouch of which he always carried on himself. But honestly, he never thought he might feel the need for it so soon. However, Nando managed to bury the temptation, at least for that moment. He looked at his watch; it was still at least an hour before Bishu would bring him his dinner. Even though he despised the fool for filling mind with garbage, Nando still looked forward to his company in this otherwise solitary confinement.

Nando didn't realise when he had dozed off until Bishu knocked at his door. It was past eight already, quite late by the local standards. Bishu had got his food, and though Nando was generally used to having a late dinner, he started eating without any fuss. Bishu waited patiently near the door as he finished his food. The food was surely home cooked and still warm. Nando felt compelled to ask whom he needed to pay for this. But Bishu didn't seem like the right person to answer that. So, he quietly finished his meal. As Bishu prepared to leave with the soiled plates, he turned back and looked at Nando as if he still had something to say. Nando had no intention to indulge in any more conversation with this chap, so he became visibly annoyed at this. But Bishu still stood there, hesitant, and awkward.

"Do you wish to say anything?" Nando asked curtly.

"Will you be able to stay here all by yourself tonight? Or else..."

"Or else, what?" Nando asked sternly.

Bishu went silent as Nando's displeasure became obvious. Nando was now convinced about the doubts that he has had about this guy, and everything made absolute sense to him. It must have been a well-sorted plan that might have already been tried and tested before on someone else, he told himself. And there were others for sure who were part of this vile plot. Bishu must be the pawn entrusted with the task to scare him off, and Nando could only guess who could come with such an idea. Or, in other words, who could want him out of that place. He did his best to camouflage the sense of angst and disgust that brewed within his heart as he spoke the words, "I will be fine, please leave. Good night."

Nando was having trouble sleeping that night – it was humid and hot as he had locked all doors and windows. His thoughts ran haywire as his stressed mind kept his wary body awake. And any distractions of any sort only added to the agony. He kept tossing and turning on the bed, trying all known tricks to fall asleep. And it was then that he heard it again. His body stiffened in alarm. He looked at the watch; it was half-past midnight. He began to sweat again, and the cold chill ran down his spine once more. His brain grew numb with fear, but he knew he could not let that happen. It's just some guy, trying to scare me away, he told himself. I can take him, or else I can just run, he thought. The voice seemed to be coming from some distance away, so he concluded that unless it was a recorded voice, there was no one outside his door. He knew he had to take a chance. So, he decided to quietly open the door and step out into the balcony with no lights, and then if he found the coast was clear, he would use the rainwater pipes next to the balcony to descend to the courtyard, and simply start running towards the school. "Whoever is behind this, they wouldn't want to hurt me," Nando consoled himself. So, he wore his glasses, put on his slippers, picked up a stick lying in the corner of the room, and slowly opened the latch on the door. He waited a moment and then gently pushed the door open. The hinges creaked aloud, breaking the calm of the night. He could hear the thumping of his heart as the cool breeze hit him on his face. It wasn't that hot outside, he realized. And the voice became louder and clearer. He looked around and waited with bated breath; not a soul could be seen or heard, apart from the voice, which seemed to come from the other end of the balcony. He looked hard, nothing could be seen through the dark, but he figured the corridor was empty. He took a deep breath and then stepped out. The moonlight seeped through the rails and formed patterns on the floor, and the rain pipe was along the bend near the steps. While he kept looking for any signs of notoriety, all that he heard was the same old voice. Today, the verses were from Lord Byron –

> *I watched thee when the foe was at our side,*
> *Ready to strike at him—or thee and me,*
> *Were safety hopeless—rather than divide*
> *Aught with one loved save love and liberty.*

> *I watched thee on the breakers, when the rock,*
> *Received our prow, and all was storm and fear,*
> *And bade thee cling to me through every shock;*
> *This arm would be thy bark, or breast thy bier.*

The door to his room suddenly banged shut behind him, shattering the silence of the night once more. Nando sprung around in shock and fell on his back. The stick fell from his hand on the marble floor, alarming some pigeons nesting on the porch. He scrambled to drag himself backwards till his back hit the wall pillar running along the balcony. And then he scampered back to his feet as a dog started howling in the lane outside. They all seem to be unhappy with the chaos this outsider was causing. Nando stood leaning against the rails, gasping for breath. To his right was his room which he was not sure was so safe anymore. Before him lay the stairs, like a dark tunnel inviting him to enter his doom. And to his left stood the wall, shrouded in mystery and mist. And from somewhere behind it, the voice continued to bellow in his usual husky baritone –

I watched thee when the fever glazed thine eyes,
Yielding my couch and stretched me on the ground
When overworn with watching, ne'er to rise
From thence if thou an early grave hadst found.

The earthquake came, and rocked the quivering wall,
And men and nature reeled as if with wine.
Whom did I seek around the tottering hall?
For thee. Whose safety first provide for? Thine.

Nando's senses were ditching him – his mind went blank, and his limbs felt numb. Yet somehow, his body continued to move unconsciously into the mist, towards the wall. And with every step, his body felt lighter. Everything around became blurry as if he was in a cloud. The voice was now clearer than ever, and it seemed it now spoke directly to him as if it could see Nando through the wood and brick and through the fear that reigned in his soul. Nando didn't even realise how close he had reached to the wall or when he had started to move aside the rubble to expose the hole in it. He couldn't feel if it hurt. It was as if his entire subconscious was only paying attention to the words that poured into his ears –

And when convulsive throes denied my breath
The faintest utterance to my fading thought,
To thee—to thee—e'en in the gasp of death
My spirit turned, oh! oftener than it ought.

Thus, much and more; and yet thou lov'st me not,
And never wilt! Love dwells not in our will.
Nor can I blame thee, though it be my lot
To strongly, wrongly, vainly love thee still.

Nando didn't realise when he had cleared a path and crawled over to the other side of the wall. He could now see what was out of bounds for everybody else. He could smell the stench of the old and hear the sounds of the ruins. But none of it seemed to elicit any reaction. It was like his mind was operating outside his body – he could feel and sense, but couldn't react or think.

"Stop…come no further," suddenly the voice echoed, breaking the monotony.

And then, the following dialogue ensued between the unknown and the lost –

"Tell me, who are you?"

"I am Nando. Who are you?"

"You don't get to ask the questions. Why have you come here?"

"I have come for my work. I am supposed to study…"

"*I don't care. Tell me, why are you in my home?*"

"The local people asked me to stay here."

"*The people! How dare they offer my house to outsiders? You should leave.*"

"I can't. My work here isn't finished."

"*And it never will be. There is nothing for you here. There is nothing for anybody here. There's only death.*"

*   *   *   *   *

The **Stranger**

"There he is", "He's going to be okay", "He needs to rest" – Nando could hear the mild murmurs around him as he slowly came back to his senses. He opened his eyes to a lot of anxious faces stooping over him. He was lying on his bed and he wasn't in pain. But as soon as the memories from previous night came flooding back to him, his body jolted in fear even in broad daylight. Mr. Ghosal walked up to his side and patted him gently on the shoulder. "What happened, my son?" Nando looked up at him blankly. "I heard the voice, Mr. Ghosal. It spoke to me. It wasn't a dream. I was right there. It was just like how you are talking to me now. Only difference is I couldn't see him. But it happened. I can still feel it," he blabbered for a while. And then he asked the question that mattered the most, "You knew about it all along, didn't you? Why didn't you tell me?" Mr. Ghosal waited patiently for him to finish. His face bore no expression whatsoever. Then he turned and looked at the people who were now flocking near the door. He lifted his hand, assuring everything was good – that was a signal for them to leave. Nando, too, looked at them and smiled. His heart was filled with gratitude for these people. He didn't know most of them and yet they had rushed to his aid when he needed it the most.

"I know what you must be feeling, son." Mr. Ghosal finally spoke once the room was empty, his voice sounding unusually calm and composed given the situation. "But I must tell you – there is no IT." Nando looked on, perplexed, as he continued to speak indifferently, "There never was. All that was there were gossip, rumours, and folklores."

"What are you talking about, I actually heard the voice? That was no dream. Can you explain that?" Nando blurted out in frustration. Mr. Ghosal had a good look at Nando; desperation and fear were writ large on the boy's face. He quietly went up to the door and closed it. And then he came back and sat down on the chair next to the bed, took a deep breath and started to tell a story that dated long back.

"Damien Wiltshire's wealth was not gold or silver, but the fertile lands of this country. At that time indigo plantation was in full swing in Bengal. There was a huge demand for this dye in the western countries, and the Englishmen were minting money from it. Mr. Damien grabbed the opportunity with both hands; he invested his savings and bought off all the farming land around the place. And then he started growing indigo on them and exporting the dye to England. He was no longer a soldier but a businessman, and he was wise enough to alter his appearance and lifestyle to mingle among the elite class. But from inside, he always remained a bloodthirsty mercenary. His way of getting the work done was through brute force and torture, not unlike most of his contemporaries. Hence, he never really became popular among the locals. An oppressing landlord was nothing new for these people. And it didn't matter much to them whether the it was an Indian or an Englishman. But the farmers had more reason to hate him than just his brutal nature. What mattered most to them were their lands – their only resource to earn a living. The indigo plantation left the soil infertile for the rest of the year, unable to produce any grain. And that was what most affected these people. The lashes hurt more when their stomachs were empty. The pain fuelled more hatred than hunger.

Damien built this mansion, which would also serve as an office for his business. The attendants were housed at the quarters at the back so that they could be available throughout the day. In the evenings, he would call professional performers from across the country and organise galas. Initially, it happened only during occasions, but as his wealth and greed grew, they became a regular affair. Tales of his debauchery became fodder for discussion among the people who knew him. This is when his son, Fernando, came to stay with him, from England. Not much is known about him. But it is said that even though he had nothing to do with his father's business, yet somehow, it was him who triggered the revolt that led to the destruction of this place. People were up in arms and neither the father nor the son survived that fateful onslaught."

Mr. Pramod Ghosal stopped at this point, but Nando waited patiently. He wasn't sure if he was done talking.

"That's it? Is that all? That makes no sense. What has any of this got to do with the voice reciting English poems from behind those walls?" Nando asked in a bitter and annoyed tone. He was done listening to stories from everyone.

Mr. Ghosal stared at him blankly for a moment and then said, "The bit I told you is history. Beyond this, all that is there is gossip. There are different versions and no proof whatsoever to support any of them. No one knows for sure what happened. But they all revolve around a single string of incidents."

"And what is that?" Nando asked impatiently.

Mr. Ghosal gave a brief pause and then said, "It was about a woman. It is said that Damien's boy got involved with a native girl. The local people didn't approve of this, but they were scared, as the Englishmen were powerful, and they owned much of the land around here. But then, one day, things went out of hand for some reason, and the villagers turned on them. It is said that Damien Wiltshire and his men killed many that night, but he couldn't save his son or himself. His son was very fond of books; the library that I told you about was his favourite place, where he spent most of his time. And so, people say that when he died in that unforeseen accident, his soul refused to leave the house. Many believe he inhabits the old library room of the house to this day, which is now beyond the wall, restricted to one and all. Once in a while, some people, like Bishu, would claim to have seen him or heard him, but we used to ignore it till the incident with Moinul. It was then that the authorities took notice, and in fear of the repercussions of the incident and anticipating the ruckus that it would create, they decided to construct that wall. They assumed that people would probably talk and debate over it for a week and then forget about it and move on, and life would get back to normal. And that is precisely what happened."

Mr. Ghosal had walked up to the window as he spoke and now stood gazing out at the distance with his arms folded across his chest. "You see, it's easy to play down or hush up an issue raised by some country fool. But with you, my son, it is all very different," he asserted grimly. "You are a learned man, an outsider with no vested interest in our affairs. If you say what you have witnessed here, everybody will believe you. And all the plans that we have made to utilise this building for something big – like turning it into a hospital or a community centre will go down the drain. I don't want that to happen; I can't let that happen." His voice grew firm and cold with every word he spoke. "That is the reason I didn't want anybody staying here in the first place, but Surjo insisted for you to be put up here since the school was occupied by his people, and I couldn't say no to him. But now I am left with no choice. There used to be an old post office just outside the village, which has been shut for over a decade now. I suppose the government never really found it very profitable to begin with. Since then, the office has remained closed, and only once a week would a van come and clear the post box, which still hangs outside the office. Anyways, there is one quarter meant for the officer next to it, and I happen to have the key to it. That too has not been opened in a long time now, but I think we can get it fixed for your stay. It's nothing compared to this manor, but I am afraid it will have to suffice for now since we are out of options here. I have sent Bishu's elder sister, Kusum, to clean the place and make it habitable. I will take your leave now to preside over its progress and ensure that you don't have to spend another night under this roof. You better get some rest now."

Saying so, Mr. Ghosal prepared to leave with Nando still caught in a mind warp. He knew he was in a mess he didn't know much about, but something seemed utterly wrong. It took him a few seconds to figure out what that was, and as soon as it occurred to him, he rushed out of his room. Mr. Ghosal, who was already down the stairs, had to stop as Nando vehemently called out his name while jumping steps to catch up with him. He was visibly in panic, with his recent misadventures taking a toll on him. "Mr. Ghosal, you are not getting the point here," Nando blurted out, completely exasperated, hands trembling in excitement. "It's not only about me. It's about all the people around here. What about them? How can you not tell them? It's about their safety, their lives. They need to know if they are in trouble."

"Let me assure you," Mr. Ghosal responded in a calm and composed voice, "This thing that you have heard has never posed any threat to anybody, and that's a fact. If he had meant harm, you wouldn't be alive right now, would you? I would request you not to talk about this to anyone so the villagers don't start doubting your state of mind. But more importantly, then you would leave us with no option to help you with your work."

Nando remained quiet as Mr. Ghosal explained himself in no uncertain terms and prepared to leave once again. But then there was something else that came to Nando's mind, which he wasn't sure was of any worth, but he had to get it off his chest anyway.

"I understand Mr. Ghosal, what you just said, and what you are trying to do here. I really do." Nando had finally managed to conjure up all the confidence he could gather to ensure that Mr. Ghosal couldn't ignore what he was about to say. "I know what I am going to say might sound weird, maybe even more than what you just narrated to me. But the fact is, and I don't know how else to say this, but from the verses I heard last night, each and every word seemed like a warning, like an indication of some terrible mishap that's coming our way. It was as if he was trying to warn us of a danger that's out there, hidden in plain sight, waiting to strike.

I don't want to interfere in your scheme of things, and I will be happy to stay away from this place any day. But I thought you should know this, that I might not be the only threat to your plans."

* * * * *

The rest of the day presented itself in peculiar discomfort for Nando, much like the overcast afternoon sky – neither much light nor any rain. He had hardly anything to pack, so that was easy. Bishu was supposed to come and fetch him by four so that they could reach and settle down in the new place before sundown. It was one and so there was ample time left, yet Nando felt impatient. He hadn't had anything to eat since morning, but surprisingly he didn't feel hungry either. In fact, he didn't feel like getting out of the bed at all, but he couldn't sleep either. He kept tossing and turning in the bed, sweating profusely, till it occurred to him that he might actually be sick. He knew that severe trauma could induce fever, anorexia etc. but never really thought he would have it for real. And while he did carry some medicines with him, he had no clue if a tablet for the common cold would be useful for this. But he knew for sure that it was a bad idea to get sick in this place when he was all by himself. And there was no way he could give up on his objective and go back home empty-handed. So, after a lot of deliberation, he decided to take half a sleeping pill and get some shut-eye till Bishu came. "That should help," he thought.

But that plan didn't work. He woke up wrapped in a blanket of darkness around him. His watch showed it was seven-thirty already, and it was evident that Bishu had not turned up as discussed, for reasons best known to him. Not even a lantern was lit, and Nando was all by himself in the same old house where he had to survive unspeakable horror the night before. It took Nando a fraction of a second to comprehend the situation, and the next moment, a terrible fear engulfed him – he lost his voice, his limbs were paralysed. His back felt stiff and cold. Sweat poured off his forehead while his throat went dry. The world suddenly seemed to have gone so quiet that he could hear the wind, and the ticking of the clock seemed like a constant knock on his numbed senses. He knew that if he stayed like this for long, he might die of his panic attack. He had to move. He had to get out of this place, into the open. But for that, first, he needed to get out of the room and walk across the corridor and down the stairs. But he wasn't sure if he could do that. Perhaps he should just lay back and wait for something terrible to happen, he thought.

But the funny thing about life is – the moment you feel like giving up on it, it gives you a nudge to push along. Nando does not know how he managed to do it, but he got out of the bed, banged the door open, and then darted across the corridor, all along singing at the top of his voice. The tough part was the stairs, as he constantly felt somebody following on his heels. He barely saved himself from falling on a couple of occasions as he flashed down the stairs and jumped into the courtyard. And then he scooted out of the gate and onto the open road. The road outside was empty, barring some stray dogs. The light at the gates continued flickering. Nando looked on both sides – no man or woman to be seen. The tea stall across the corner was shut, the rickshaw stand was empty. All the houses along the road had their doors closed. Humans seemed to have ceased to exist in that village. There was only the wind – a howling, cold gush of air that blew the dust around in small circles. Nando felt it kiss his sweaty, stiff neck as the world began to dwindle in front of his eyes. He started running again in the direction of the schoolhouse, but he couldn't go far. The otherwise civil canines on the road suddenly began to bark and chase him from every direction. Nando stopped running, but they still kept coming at him. Their jaws were wide open, and their eyes looked red. Nando had nowhere else to go but back inside the gates. He could barely breathe when he stepped back into the courtyard. His legs were giving up on him as he found himself surrounded by the dogs. He was ready to resign himself to his fate, but surprisingly the animals never crossed the gates. They remained outside, barking at him while he crashed on the grass.

* * * * *

The next few minutes seemed like an eternity, as Nando laid on that grass, apparently both helpless and hopeless, looking at the sky. The dogs continued to bark a few feet away from him, albeit outside the limits of the house. Their voices died down only once the sky opened up. They dispersed and ran hitherto to find shelter as the rain started falling in big drops on the ground and on Nando's face. It prompted him to close his eyes as he slowly sat himself up. He ran his fingers through his hair and then looked up at the empty balcony. He could see his door still open. He quietly got back to his feet and made his way inside.

He slowly walked up the stairs, with steady, assured steps till he reached the first-floor balcony. He spared a glance at the wall and then calmly turned left and walked up to his room. He kept the door open as he picked up his bag and reached inside without even looking. When he pulled his hand out, it held a pouch of brown, shredded grass. Without any hurry or panic, he slowly rolled himself a smoke by mixing the contents of that pouch with tobacco. He held a burning match to the pointy end and took a long, slow drag. And then he turned and sat on his bed, reclined himself on the pillow, and let out a huge, dense puff of smoke filling the air with a pungent stench of marijuana.

Nando relaxed and indulged in every drag he took as if it could be his last. His mind was now empty, devoid of any worries, fears, or concerns. He felt lighter, not just in his head but in his soul. He quietly got off the bed. His feet were steady. He was clear about what he was going to do. He picked up his torch from his backpack and stepped out onto the balcony. He had earlier noticed a thin iron rod lying along the corner. He calmly picked it up and started walking down the corridor, as it continued to pour outside. He walked all the way up to the solitary wall that stood there blocking his path. And then, he picked up the rod and hit it so hard against the wall that pieces of splinter and bricks crumbled and fell onto the floor. But Nando didn't stop. The rubble at his feet continued to grow until the hole in the wall was big enough for him to pass without getting on his knees.

"Stop…come no further," the voice sounded from afar. The pitch was higher this time, and the tone was meaner. A conversation ensued again, but a different one, as Nando didn't allow being asked all the questions this time.

"I will unless you tell me who you are."

"As I said earlier, you don't get to ask the questions here."

"And you don't get to have an opinion. You are not supposed to exist. You are an abomination. And a criminal. You have killed someone."

"Tell me stranger – if you chase a kitten and it gets run over by a car, would you say you have killed it?"

"I would, because it's fear that pushed him under the wheels."

"Wel, in my defence, the kitten was in my kitchen."

"You don't have a kitchen. And this is not your house anymore. You are dead."

"How dare you!"

"How dare I what? Tell the truth? Well, I guess it is about time."

"And what truth will that be?"

"That I am not an outsider here, you are. Or you were. Whatever, but you can't tell me to leave this place. I will stay here as long as I wish, okay?"

"And die here too, if it leads to that? Like that boy?"

"Are you threatening me?"

"Do I need to? I thought you were smarter than that."

"Don't forget you died here too."

"Yes, by a bunch of haggard people who value their lands more than somebody's life."

"I hope you hear yourself when you say that. Do you remember the excuse you made a minute ago for killing someone?"

"Listen, boy, the only reason I am still tolerating you is because I think you are a person of reasonably higher intelligence than the rest."

"I guess I should be flattered, but what makes you so sure about it?"

"I heard what you said to that old prick Ghosal. It was wise of you to try and make sense of the things I implied."

"You mean the poetry you recite, which keeps me awake all night long."

"And you seem to be the only one to make sense of it. That was impressive. I think talking to you will not be a complete waste of my time."

"Well, I am sure you have loads of it to spare."

"How about you?"

"I am not going anywhere unless we are done here."

"Very well then. Step in."

Thus, Nando entered the old library room in the restricted section of the building in the middle of night, upon the insistence of a ghost of an Englishman who had lived there a hundred years ago. And all this happened after he had smoked a handsome quantity of weed all by himself.

So, this part of the story might seem insane and absurd to most. And no amount of reasoning can make it look real for those who don't believe. But for the sake of the tale, we need to assume that all of this is true. Because otherwise, we will never get to know the person behind the voice that echoed around in an empty manor on long and lonely nights.

It belonged to a young English boy who came to India during the nineteenth century and could never return. This is his story, in his own words, with some unwarranted interruptions by a young Bengali guest.

* * * * *

The **Conversation**

"So, how long have you lived here?"

"Living is for those who are alive. I stay here."

"But this was your home, right?"

"It still is. Because I am still here."

"Dead people cannot have a claim on any part of the living world."

"They are not supposed to exist either…but here we are."

"Existing is what most dead people do, sometimes even when they are alive."

"Are you mocking me?" Do you think all this is a joke?"

"No, this isn't a joke, but neither is interfering in someone else's business."

"You are staying in my home – what do you think you are doing? Visiting or interfering?"

"You were staying in my country – what do you think you were doing? Visiting or interfering?"

"You weren't even born then. How was this your country?"

"You are not even alive now. How is this your home?

At this juncture in their conversation, a tense silence descended upon them for a brief moment, before the phantom spoke again.

"My name is Fernando Wiltshire, or rather, was."

"That's okay. Your name doesn't have to die with you. In fact, part of it lives in mine. What an irony! Anyway, go ahead and tell me more about you?"

"And why do you think would I do that?"

"Because I guess you want to, and I am here."

"I was born in the winter of 1829 in a small village in Ealing, about thirty kilometres to the west of London. Our family had migrated from the bitterly cold and barren northern parts of the kingdom, even before I was born. They wanted a better life for themselves and for us. So, the men would stay away for months trying to make a livelihood in the city while we grew up learning to read and write. We all lived together in a small wooden house, where the women would breed cattle and try to grow vegetables in the backyard. The neighbourhood mostly comprised of migrants like us, and it was filthy. The people and the cattle littered the roads alike, and the men who stuck around would get drunk and fight all

day long. There were no schools, and neither did our parents have any time for us. So, we almost had the entire day to do whatever we felt like."

"Our eldest sister would wake us up, make us breakfast and then we were on our own. I had two cousin brothers, and between us, we had one cycle and a pony. We would hop, skip, and jump to the forest and hills surrounding the village. In stark contrast to the condition of the human settlements, the countryside was unbelievably beautiful. The valleys, the rocks, and the lakes form some of the best memories of my childhood. I would sit beneath a tree with a pencil and a paper, trying to make a sketch or practising a few words, while my brothers would loiter around aimlessly, being up to no good. My mother would often complain that my brothers were growing up to be exactly like the other men of the village. They would climb the trees, swim in the lake or race along the undulating planes on their ponies. I was the youngest of the lot, and not being a very healthy kid, I usually refrained from participating. And since I was weak and small and didn't quite share their enthusiasm, they would often bully me. But I never complained, fearing that more would follow. But this one time, it went a bit too far. And that one incident would change my life forever."

"I guess even as a kid you weren't very likeable!" Nando quipped cheekily.

"No, they were just as annoying as you are!" Fernando retorted sourly, as he turned his back to Nando and continued with his story.

"It was winter. Every morning we would wake up to a thin layer of snow upon everything around us. Our men were back home for the holidays, with presents and gifts for us, so the women and kids were all happy alike. My father had joined Her Highness's Royal British Army and had travelled to far and distant lands across the seven seas. His brothers, on the other hand, were working as labour in a workhouse in London, in conditions which they described as a living nightmare. In the evenings, we would shut the doors and windows, make a fire and gather around to listen to their stories. One would tell stories of valour and honour, while the other would share tales of struggle and corruption.

The Great War with the French had left the empire in an advanced state of decay. Though the war was won, the cost was steep. Some later said that the foundation of the largest empire the world has seen was laid with that victory. But in reality, it resulted in a nation plagued with a thousand diseases. The landowners controlled the fates of a million people. The end of the war presented them with the opportunity to import cheap foreign grain. Intrigued by this fact, they introduced the Corn Laws to make sure that their purchasing power wouldn't decline.

As per these laws, heavy import duties were levied on wheat to ensure that the price of home-grown food didn't fall beyond a certain level. And these taxes continued to grow steeper with time. The condition of the poor was appalling. Manufacturing wages were higher than agriculture, and hence many people were forced to migrate to the industrial and urban centres, leaving their homes and families behind. In 1830, farm labourers in Kent and Sussex broke agricultural machinery, fearing it would cause unemployment. The riots were called the Swing Riots because they were supposedly led by a man named Captain Swing. As a result of the riots, four men were hanged and fifty-two were transported to Australia. At the time, convict ships were sent from England directly to the colony of Tasmania, then known as Van Diemen's Land. Till 1832, Britain was ruled primarily by an oligarchy of landowners. My father had travelled to Australia as an escort to those prisoners in during late 1830s, before being sent to India almost a decade later."

"I thought the incident you mentioned involved your brothers and not your father."

"Why can't you just be a little patient?"

"Because I don't want you to bore me to death tonight. Anyway, carry on."

"My father deeply regretted the fact that he wasn't around when we were growing up and that we had to manage on our own when he should have been there to hold our hands. To make up for that, he used to bribe us with gifts from various parts of the world. That time he got me an ivory casket, studded with stones, which he had gotten from a tribal chief. None of us had ever seen anything like it. That became my very special possession, something I proudly showed off to one and all, much to the envy of my kin. Uncle Martin could manage much less for his children, so my brothers

grew jealous. We all were kids, and though in our hearts we knew love and hate, joy and sorrow, we were yet to learn the complex ways of the mind. So, while I didn't feel their pain, they didn't share my happiness. I started to ignore them and spend time with my possession, wandering on my own and collecting little pieces of junk that would fascinate me. I started to describe things, small and special, that only I used to notice, which intrigued people to pay more attention to me than hearing about the naughty escapades of the rest. My brothers would feel left out, obsolete, unethically defeated and hence they wanted me to suffer. So, one day they told me that they had discovered a hidden cave on the other side of the hill and were going to excavate it. They invited me to join. I was excited, and it wasn't very tough to get permission from my father. I happily rode pillion on my younger brother's bicycle. He paddled hard to keep up with my elder brother's pony as it galloped over the fields and across the hill, where we used to play hide and seek when we were young. We rode all the way to the lake on the other side, where they decided to take a dip. I wasn't prepared as they had not informed me about any such plan. They stripped down to their boxers and went into the lake and kept calling me to join. In fact, they said they were ready to go skinny dipping so that I don't feel bad. And they indeed took off their underwear and threw them on the shore. They insisted so much that I took off my clothes as well and entered the water naked."

"Sorry to interrupt again, but I honestly don't like where this story is headed. No offence, but I am not interested in the details of a gay orgy." Nando interrupted him with an abrupt chuckle.

"Do you even listen to the words coming out of your mouth?" Fernando rebuked him with utter disgust, as he threw his hands in the air and floated away to the corner before he started talking again.

"And we swam there until we were tired and far from the shore. Then they suggested a game to see who could hold their breath the longest underwater. I guess I was able to do that for hardly about a minute or so. And when I came back up, I saw my brothers racing away with their clothes and mine too. I was left behind – angry, scared, alone and naked. As it grew dark, I stepped out of the water, ashamed and cold. I could have died out there that day. But as I made my way through the forests, my eyes fell on her. She was about my age, a bit shorter than me, with blonde hair and brown eyes. She was out collecting firewood, it seemed, and she was looking straight at me when I saw her. I ran and hid behind a rock and prayed she would go away. But she didn't. Instead, I heard her voice as the cloak she wore came flying down on me. 'You will be fine, don't be scared,' she said from a distance. That was the sweetest voice I had ever heard, and that was the best thing I had ever been told. But I didn't see her again. She was gone when I came out. All that remained of her was a memory and the cloak she had offered.

I brought it back with me and would always carry it along. I would look at it for hours – its texture was unusually, and its colour was unique. It would have been blue originally, but now it was a weird shade of grey, unlike anything they could ever weave in the looms. It became an obsession. As I grew up, I continued to learn and research the textile industry – how they made clothes and how they made dyes to add colour to it. At one point I decided to take up my passion as a profession as well. And luck presented me with the best opportunity one could ask for."

Fernando stopped talking at this point, as he noticed that his passionate story-telling has acted as a lullaby for Nando, who had curled up on the books and was now asleep like a baby.

* * * * *

Nando must have dozed off in the wee hours of the night in spite of this inexplicable and extraordinary encounter. But as the distorted memories of the night returned to haunt him in his subconscious mind, he jolted out of his slumber in a cold sweat, his heart pounding and fists clenched. It was quite late in the morning, and everything around seemed absolutely normal. He was lying on the table in a dirty old room with books scattered all around him. He still had his torch beside him, and it worked fine as he pressed the switch. As much as he could remember, he never actually used it during the night, even though it could have proven useful on a couple of occasions. He rubbed his eyes and looked around again. There were no signs of anything remotely out of place, apart from him.

"Must be the weed," he told himself. But it still felt weird all the same.

As his fear subsided over the next few minutes, the other instincts started to kick in. He was famished and had had nothing to drink since last evening. He looked around. There was nothing but books all around him, on the tables and the shelves, covered in a thin layer of dust. He picked one up; the pages still seemed crisp and warm as well. He looked around once more and then stepped out into the corridor. He stepped out of the hole carefully and walked up to his room as quietly as he could. He kept looking around every now and then as he did. But the moment he entered the room, he nearly jumped out of his skin, as he noticed someone hunching on the floor near the bed.

"Where have you been?" Horen asked curtly, even as Nando was trying to get over the shock. He had to spare a few moments to gather himself, and then he retorted sharply, "I think I should be the one asking that."

Horen had stood up in the meantime. He now turned and looked Nando in the eye. He probably wasn't expecting such a curt response from the otherwise demure lad. But he was smart enough to realise his mistake immediately.

"Pardon me, please," he uttered politely and then continued to speak in a sombre tone as he said, "I am not in my element today. Please get ready. Surjo has asked me to escort you outside Damanpur."

Nando turned in astonishment. He wasn't expecting this.

"What do you mean? Who said I am leaving?" he asked in an agitated tone.

"Surjo did. Something terrible has happened. You should leave immediately." Horen iterated more assertively this time.

"I am not leaving without my answers." Nando refused to budge.

"Ok, then come with me, please," Horen asked him, now visibly distraught. "You can see for yourself, and decide if you still want to stick around."

*   *   *   *   *

The **Tragedy**

It was like a funeral at the schoolhouse. Men and women of all ages thronged the courtyard. Their faces were writ with tension and fear, but what they felt within was pure, unadulterated rage. Their indistinct murmurs filled the atmosphere with an uncanny unpleasantness. As Nando stepped inside, people all but spared a glance and then turned their heads the other way. Their actions looked animated; their movements were restless. Suddenly, a loud cry emerged from somewhere close, piercing the uneasy calm. And then it slowly went silent again. Nando looked around as if he was sleepwalking, and it was all but a nightmare. He could barely breathe, his body was soaked in sweat, and his heart was racing ahead of his mind. His legs refused to carry him any further, while an unknown anxiety slowly started to numb his senses. It's not real – he tried to convince himself. But it was. He was not so dumb to not realise it. Nando stood there shaking in pain and fear until somebody called his name. He looked up. It was Surjo.

"What are you still doing here? You were supposed to leave, didn't Horen meet you?" he uttered rudely, his disgust evident on his face.

"Yes, he met me. But I told him I can't leave now; I have not even started my work. Then he brought me here," Nando barely mumbled.

Surjo gave him a cold stare, trying to gauge his verity, while Nando continued to look around disconcertedly.

"Bring him inside," Surjo muttered to his aides and turned around and left. Two of his men followed him, almost dragging Nando with them.

Surjo walked straight down the corridor, steering a path among the people who flocked the narrow passage, followed by his men. The last room on the left was where all the attention was focused. A bunch of people swarmed outside that door, but the room itself seemed empty from outside. The people bore a blank look, with a ghastly petrified or exasperated expression, as if they were zombies. They lined the passage like a troop of undead and made way as the men approached the door.

The faint cry Nando had heard outside grew louder with every step they took. Surjo paused as he reached the door. He shut his eyes for a moment, let off a deep breath and then stepped inside. Baffled and confused, Nando followed suit. Women sat in a circle on the floor, trying to control one in particular who was crying and wailing like she was possessed. In front of her lay a body covered in a cloth with bloodstains. But the person was alive. It was a girl. She moaned and cried as her limbs twitched in pain. It was hard to guess her age from her face, which was swollen and bruised. Her eyes could barely be seen. Blood clots covered her lips and ears. Her hair was torn at places; bite marks could be seen on her neck and throat. The rest of her body remained covered, but it wasn't tough to assume that it had been deformed in a fire. The air was heavy with a pungent smell of burnt flesh mixed in sweat, tears and blood. Nando remained frozen for a few moments till the situation loomed on his senses, and then he rushed outside, to the window at the edge of the corridor and flung it open with one ravage push. He leaned out and tried to soak in the air, but the smell still clouded his senses. He closed his eyes and tried to reign in his emotions, but the face of that girl kept coming back to haunt him. He tried to swallow what choked his throat, but the lump kept crawling up. He clenched the window grill as his head started to spin. His bowels contorted, his eyes dilated, and then he started throwing up.

A minute or two passed by as Nando stood there gasping, before he felt Surjo's cold jittery hands touching his shoulders. Nando turned and looked him in the eye. They were moist, and yet a fire raged in them.

Nando's voice cracked as he mumbled the words, "Is she still breathing?"

"Yes, but not for long." Surjo's voice seethed with anger and pain as he spoke.

"What happened to her?" Nando asked softly. Though his mind was fully aware of the answer, it was yet to sink in his heart.

Surjo's eyes seemed to pierce into his soul as his cold voice hissed, "Do you really not understand? Are you dumb or just acting stupid? Or do you want me to spell it out for you to believe it had happened?"

Nando kept looking at him quietly, with literally no expression on his face.

Surjo was exasperated, but he knew he needed to talk as well. And Nando was the only person around who wouldn't judge him for being weak. So, he spoke, looking away so nobody could see his face.

"The girl you saw inside is Kusum. She is Bishu's sister. This poor girl was assigned the task to clean the old, empty post office where you were supposed to be shifted. And guess what she found there when she went to do her job? A few bastards, who didn't mind raping and ravaging a fourteen-year-old girl, choking her and gagging her and biting off her skin all at the same time, making a feast out of her flesh. And then, when they were done, they poured kerosene on her while she would still be begging to be left alone, and they tried to burn her alive to silence her mouth. And had it not been for some kind and concerned man who noticed the smoke and informed us, she would have become a carcass by now."

Nando tried to stop Surjo halfway, as his senses tried to reject the visuals his mind was imagining. His stomach began to twitch once again, and it felt like every last drop of his body fluid started pouring out of his mouth. Surjo held Nando by his wrists till he had dropped on his knees, his grip tightening with every word he spoke while Nando convoluted and vomited until his throat began to bleed. He might have collapsed if Surjo's associates hadn't pulled him away for some aid.

* * * * *

Nando might have lost consciousness for some time, but he can't say for sure, as his mind had stopped registering the reality for a while. He woke up to find himself lying on a bench in what seemed like a classroom. He realised he was still in the school, as the wailing could still be faintly heard through the closed doors and windows. He was not alone, though. Surjo was there, so was Horen and Mr. Ghosal. He noticed that even Das babu, the jovial owner of Annapurna Cabin, was also there. Others present were also known faces, whom he had seen on the campus when he arrived, but he couldn't recall all their names. He remembered Fatik, however, who stood in a corner dejectedly. They were all angry. Everything about them, from their faces to their fists, manifested what they were feeling inside.

Nando's head felt heavy as he tried to pull himself up.

"Here, have this. It will help." Das babu handed him a small cup of tea.

Nando nodded and smiled as he took the cup and sipped at it. It indeed felt good. Das babu slowly walked back to where Surjo stood in the company of a few senior members of the community engaged in what looked like a heated debate. Das babu whispered something to him, and then Surjo turned and looked at Nando. Nando cringed as he remembered their sordid interaction earlier in the day. He looked away, trying to ignore Surjo as he slowly walked towards him.

"I am sorry, Nando, for how I behaved earlier. I hope you understand, given the circumstances, it is tough to get hold of one's emotions, and I suppose I got carried away. None of this is your fault, after all," he exclaimed as he came and stood near his friend.

"It's okay," Nando uttered with a plain face and then asked, "How is the girl?"

"Still breathing," Surjo said, his voice choking as he spoke. "Why don't you pray to your God for her life. He seems to have stopped listening to us."

"There is a doctor attending to her, right?" Nando asked in genuine concern.

"No, my friend! There is no doctor around here, at least not anymore," Surjo uttered dejectedly. "The last one left for holidays and never came back." He paused for a brief moment and then continued, "It's our own doing. We blocked the roads to stop anything or anybody from breaching our perimeter, be it the government, police, or even the media. We thought this way we could protect our lands and our people. But we were wrong.

Our enemy is strong. They have unmatched resources at their disposal. And they have decided to use intimidation as a policy. They expect us to beg for help, and then they would call out their conditions, and we would have no option but to agree. In one way, they would use the media to portray that they are helping us while lawlessness prevails here. And on the other hand, they would barter our rights in exchange for the assistance we need to save the girl. And the people guilty of doing that to a girl would never be punished."

"Why?" Nando couldn't help himself from asking the question.

Surjo looked at him with his cold, steely eyes once again as he explained, "Because the master doesn't kill a stooge."

An eerie silence descended upon the room once he had said those words.

"But who do you think could have done something like this?" Nando asked.

"No one from around here, I can guarantee that," Surjo uttered ferociously.

"But you know all the roads in and out of this village have been blocked, and you have armed guards posted at most places, you yourself said that. Then how the hell would outsiders enter the place and get away after doing something like this?" Nando asked again.

"You reached, didn't you?" Surjo answered stoically. Nando was stunned.

"I could reach only because I had help from…" he mumbled before the obvious conclusion dawned upon him.

Surjo pondered for a while and shared a quick glance with the rest of the folks. Every face in the room looked grim. And then he spoke, "I suppose we now know how this could have happened. While none of us saw this coming, we should have been prepared. The storm had caused considerable damage to most of the structures in its way, which included a couple of artificial blockades we had created. Some of these places were in remote corners around the village, and we can't man all the points all the time. And as it is, most of the manpower that we had was busy for the last couple of days in rescue and recovery. The perpetrators utilised this window of opportunity to enter the village and set up a hide-out in that old post office. But they couldn't have done that on their own. They were aware that nobody ever goes to the post office. Only someone local could have provided this information. And the same person would have also helped them reach there unnoticed. It was just unfortunate that Kusum had to go there. But it is also true that otherwise, we would have never known about this."

Everybody in the room quietly listened until Surjo had stopped talking. And once he was done, they continued to stand like puppets without flinching a muscle. But their eyes now looked suspiciously at the person standing next to them. Nando could easily gauge that the situation was going to get uglier in the days to come. And he was finally convinced that he had no choice but to get out of Damanpur before that.

"Now what?" one of the guys finally managed to ask.

"Now it's time for revenge," Surjo said without breaking a sweat.

"We must not do something hastily," came a voice from behind. Everybody's head turned in an instant. It was Mr. Ghosal who had spoken.

"What do you mean by hasty, Sir? Isn't this a big enough issue for you?" Sumitra could no longer control her emotions and retorted with sheer disgust in her voice.

"That's not what I meant, dear. I just wanted to say that we should plan our next actions carefully." Mr. Ghosal tried to explain.

"Why should we? Let's find these guys and make an example of them. So that no one ever dares do something like that again." Surjo fumed.

"And I think that way we can send a message to those godforsaken people who think they are the owners of our lives and our lands," blurted Horen. While others cheered at that comment, Mr. Ghosal remained silent.

"I think we must listen to what he has to say," Das babu intervened.

"Yes, I think you should." Nando, too, supported the thought, hoping to get himself an opportunity to leave.

Surjo looked at both of them and remained silent.

"Please go ahead, Mr. Ghosal," Das babu insisted.

"Look, nobody feels worse than me. What that little girl had to suffer; I feel somewhat responsible for it as I was the one who assigned her the task to go to that place. And God knows how much I want to see those guys punished. But the fact is we do not even know where they are? I am sure they would not be sitting around waiting for us. And the other thing I am sure about is this was probably not on their agenda because Kusum was not supposed to go there under normal circumstances. So, we shouldn't let ourselves be distracted by this and try to find out the real reason why they were there? What were they trying to do? What was their real plan?"

He paused for a moment, but everybody kept silent.

"Go on, Mr. Ghosal." Surjo broke the silence, still with his back to the entire crowd. "I am listening."

Mr. Ghosal looked at the blank faces around the room. Das babu gave a slight nod. Mr. Ghosal cleared his throat and continued, "I think they were here for some other reason, to do something else. Something that we are yet to know, which might trigger panic or problem, or both. This incident would have foiled that plan. But they will still succeed if we now become irrational in our response and lose focus from the bigger picture."

"And what do you think this rational approach should be?" Sumitra asked vehemently.

"I think we first need to arrange for her to be taken to the hospital, and then we can sit and decide what to do next." Mr. Ghosal kept it short.

"So, this is your plan? We just open our defences and let them in, and give up the girl, so that they can put the blame for the entire incident on us? And then they will use their media to malign everything we have done, distort the facts, and use their strength to crush our opposition and yet be deemed as the one doing justice. Is that what you want?" Surjo muttered curtly as he turned to face the elderly gentleman.

"But there, at least the girl would have a chance to live. And if she testifies against them, the media would believe us, and then we can pressurise them to bring the perpetrators to justice." Mr. Ghosal was almost pleading now.

"Given where we are and what we stand for – you seem to have an awful lot of faith in our government, I must say," Surjo commented, the hint of sarcasm evident in his voice.

"What do you mean, Surjo?" Mr. Ghosal was aghast. Das babu came forward and put his hand on his shoulders. Surjo remained silent.

"The moment we give her up, they will kill her. Don't you get it? They won't let her give a statement," Sumitra retorted.

"She would die here as well, probably before the night ends," Horen uttered what was undoubtedly in the back of everybody's mind.

Everybody fell quiet once more.

"We can't do anything to help her. Neither can we prove what happened to her. Does that seem like the right choice?" Das babu asked again.

"Why can't we get justice for her our way?" Horen asked in exasperation.

"Because what any one of us says doesn't matter, none of it. The only thing that would have mattered is her official statement." Nando interjected at this point, seeing that the conversation was headed nowhere.

"You stay out of it. This does not concern you," Sumitra spoke again. "Had it not been for you, maybe none of this would have happened at all."

"So now it is his fault, is it?" Mr. Ghosal spoke again. "Everything is everybody else's fault. Nobody is asking how the goons managed to enter the village on your watch." He seemed to have lost his patience finally.

Surjo turned around sharply to this statement, and Horen had to rush in to avoid further escalation of the situation. Das babu tried to pull Mr. Ghosal away while Sumitra sat holding her head in her palms. Utter chaos was about to erupt when Nando's faint voice was heard again, and everybody fell silent as soon as he uttered the words, "I can help. There is a way."

* * * * *

It was almost sundown when Nando stepped out into the open with Surjo. A day that dawned in gore and blood was coming to an end. It had claimed a life, but the indomitable human spirit now sought justice. Nando knew this was not his fight; he knew that as well as anybody else. And he was sure very soon he would be gone, leaving the people and this place behind forever. Even if he hadn't offered to help, it wouldn't have mattered much because nobody expected it. He would have been back to the mundane comfort of his home in Kolkata and explored other ways to fulfil his objective. And Damanpur would have carried on the way it always has – on its own. But that was not to be.

As everyone feared, Kusum didn't survive much longer. Her body lost the battle with pain. But her battle for justice wasn't over yet. Before she breathed her last, her statement was captured in a portable video recorder that

Nando offered. He had carried it with him in case he ever needed to record something on tape but could never have imagined it would be this. He demonstrated how to use it, and Sumitra did the rest. She stood right next to Kusum's deathbed as she narrated her ordeal. Once it was done, she had quietly walked up to Nando and handed it over. She didn't speak to anyone for a long time after that, and nobody dared to disturb her either. Her distress was evident in her calm.

Bishu had been given a high dose of sedatives to put him to sleep, so Nando could not say his goodbyes. Surjo gave him a hug, his eyes blurring with tears, proving that the man was not without a heart after all. Sumitra was way too upset to say anything; she just folded her hands with a slight bow as a faint thank you slipped through her trembling lips. And then Nando made his way back to the mansion. He was absolutely sure in his mind about what he needed to do. He walked straight up to his room and got to work immediately. His eyes were burning, but he had no time to waste. He copied the footage on his laptop and then made a copy on a disc. He kept the disc inside a drawer of the table, as he had told Surjo he would. But he still left a letter beneath the jug, just in case he forgot. He then got to packing his stuff. Horen was supposed to pick him up early in the morning and shepherd him to the highway bus stand. And then all this would be behind him. Surjo had promised that Nando's name wouldn't appear anywhere irrespective of whatever form the agitation would take. Nando trusted his words completely. After all, that was what had given him the courage to come all this way for a college project, which felt like a really silly and stupid idea in hindsight. And then he was reminded of Bishu, probably because he had always thought of that boy as a fool. But to think of how much that little boy has had to suffer had a humbling effect on Nando. Most men wouldn't be able to endure half of what he has survived, he thought in his mind.

All these thoughts had kept him distracted while he packed his bag. But then he suddenly noticed that he was also carrying his voice recorder and a weird idea struck him. He looked at his watch; it was almost ten-thirty. He had an entire night in front of him, and sleep was going to elude him for sure. So, he came up with an ingenious way to make good use of that time.

He quickly finished packing but kept the recorder handy. He then left the room, shutting the door behind him so it would seem that it was locked from inside. Then he quietly made his way to the wall and sneaked in through the hole, covering it behind him. Then he lit his torch with a deft touch and made his way inside the library once again. He was confident he wasn't going to be alone, and he was right.

*   *   *   *   *

The **Departure**

"*I see that you are back. Didn't expect that.*"

"Weird as it may sound, it seems that this is the safest place for me at the moment."

"*Isn't that the funniest thing I have heard since my death! But I suppose you are right.*"

"What do you mean? Do you know what's going on out there?"

"*You see, I experience time and space differently. How else do you think I gave you the warning?*"

"I wish you had been more explicit in your words; we could have saved a life."

"*I can do only as much as I am destined to.*"

"If you say so. Any other warning that I should know about today?"

"*Nothing from your present, I am afraid.*"

"I guess then we have nothing else to talk about anymore, so why don't you continue with your story? I could surely use the distraction."

"Okay, if you so insist. In the year 1841, we received a penny post from my father. He was well, and he was in London. He said that he had been allotted an employee's quarter in the city and asked us to join him there. That letter came as a breath of fresh air. I was tired of that small place I called home and the crude people who surrounded me. The books I read had opened my windows to the far wide world that lay outside my village, a world I was dying to explore and experience first-hand. So, I left Ealing and started the journey to find myself. The only part that pained me was leaving my mother behind. She loved me the most, but her responsibilities didn't allow her to abandon the rest of the family.

During that time, London used to be the largest city in Europe. And it continued to grow at a phenomenal rate, in congruence with the growing expanse of the British East India Company across the globe. And along with it grew the disparity between the different classes of people who lived there. While their numbers grew in leaps and bounds, the government found it tough to provide the basic amenities to the people. Villas were built for the wealthy, while the poor were sheltered in filthy, dark, row houses. My house was across a narrow alley leading up to a shipping yard in one of the less populated parts of the city. The lane was lined with minuscule two-storeyed apartments made of wood and red brick, each of which looked absolutely similar. A small flight of stairs led to the front door, behind which the dreams and struggles of the family remained hidden alike. The first-floor room next to the attic was my kingdom, and the adjacent balcony was my escapade. I would stand there and watch the sun set over the Thames, and the beauty of that sight would linger upon my senses long after it's gone. Dim halogen lamps would light the streets at night, while chimneys all over the town would belch coal smoke, giving rise to the infamous London smog that would engulf the entire city during the after-hours. The street sweepers would toil hard to clean the roads of stinking horse manure. Drunkards, beggars, pickpockets, and prostitutes would line the roads, exposing the dark underbelly of the city that was widely touted to be achieving the pinnacle of the industrial revolution. The reality was that the wealth that was created didn't trickle down to the ones at the bottom of the food chain. The poor and the working class lived in miserable conditions. Working women were a big taboo in society. Sexual discrimination was at large, and women were not allowed access to higher positions. A highly male chauvinistic society restricted their job profile to physical labour. And the poor pay would sometimes force them to stoop even lower to maintain their contribution to their households until their children were old enough to earn. As late as the 1850s, the judiciary dabbled with the laws as what would be an ideal hour that a woman or a child could devote to the workplace. And all this to bring meagre quantities of low-quality food to the table daily after paying an exorbitant amount of price for the same in the Saturday night markets where the dealers were able to off-load their unsaleable produce."

Fernando stopped at this moment and turned to look at Nando, who sat flipping through the pages of a book while his eyes remained fixated on the floating storyteller.

"Are you already bored today? It's still early."

"Not really, these are all very interesting facts. Actually, this book here has the exact same pictures of London from that era"

"The book you are holding is a travel journal for Africa."

"Okay, I am sorry. But you need to know your audience, buddy; you can't sell water to a whale."

"What do you mean? You know all about the nineteenth-century London society?"

"No, I don't. But I do know about the poverty that you want me to picture."

"I can't say which one is more frustrating – back when I was talking to these walls or now that I am talking to you."

"Are these the only two contenders, or there were other times as well when you had felt equally miserable and helpless?"

"As a matter of fact, I did. When my mother died, a part of me died too. She was the only thing that connected me to the

outside world. I would visit her as often as I could. Now with her gone, nothing around seemed to matter anymore. So, when my father urged me to accompany him to India, I had no reason to refuse. India – the land of monks, magicians, and maharajas – where people rode elephants and camels and worshipped stones and trees. For the British Empire, it was just another colony; a money-minting machine of a million people whom they considered inferior and undeserving in all aspects. I had read all about this place, but it was hard for me to believe that a civilisation as old as this would produce nothing but farmers, labourers, and mindless rulers who had lost an entire country trying to settle petty rivalries. But the fact is, when I came here, that is exactly what I saw. People were busy with their individual lives and their individual problems. All were busy fighting their individual battles in the confines of their homes while their lives were dictated at others' terms. Even their dreams weren't allowed to breach the threshold they were confined to.

People were poor and uneducated. Sickness ran at large. Those who didn't die of hunger or managed not to get killed by the Company usually succumbed to malaria, cholera, or some other disease. And this I had a problem with. Though I knew these people meant nothing to me, they were human beings all the same – flesh and blood and bone, and they would surely mean a lot to someone else out there. But the times were such that morality seemed to have taken the backseat, and the only things that mattered were business and power.

And I was well aware I was on the wrong side on this one. My father was partisan to this entire enterprise. He owned lands and labour involved in indigo cultivation. I was used to hearing discussions in our drawing room about torture meted out to the natives by people I knew very well. They were respected members of my fraternity, friends of my father and yet I couldn't help but cringe when they would laugh while talking about these cruelties. When I look back at the time, I feel ashamed that I didn't do anything about it. I didn't even voice my objection to these atrocities. I guess I was in love with the dye, and so I stayed quiet while innocent blood was spilt. It's been a century since I have died, but that guilt still haunts me.

My father would often send me to supervise these lands and ensure that the farmers gave nothing less than their hundred percent on the field. I would look forward to these opportunities to sneak out from the bungalow and breathe some fresh air. It was during one of these trips that it happened.

"What happened?" Nando asked impatiently as Fernando paused for a moment.

"Don't worry, Nando," Fernando quipped sarcastically. *"It is too early in the story for me to die."*

"I was on my way back from a neighbouring village after checking on our fields. It was a hot summer afternoon, and I was on horseback. I got held up a bit and was late to start that day. But I was barely trudging along, soaked in sweat.

And that wasn't helpful as I was losing daylight fast. I had run out of drinking water, and there were no houses to be seen nearby. So, I decided to go through the woods, which would save me some time and also give me some shade in the heat. That road was only used by those who went into the forest to gather wood and otherwise remained empty. Common people usually avoided this route, as it passed through the old swamp of Bakultola, and the place had a bad reputation regarding more than one thing.

The path was laced with dense green foliage on either side and was only wide enough for a single cart to pass at a time. It was, however, comparatively easier to ride a horse down the road, as it could gallop a little faster on it. I was now sure that I would make up for the lost time, so I decided to stop for a while near a pond. My skin had turned red in the heat, and I needed to refill water for the onward journey. It was a quiet and lonely place; not another soul could be seen anywhere near. I rolled up my sleeves and took off my boots as I quietly stepped into the water. It was cold. It immediately soothed my throbbing veins, and my eyes closed by themselves.

I don't remember how long I stood there inhaling the fresh, fragrant air, and I could feel the energy seeping back into me. Then I took out my container and dipped it in the water to fill. I casually watched the bubbles it made as the water poured itself into it. I guess I got a bit lost as my senses were all relaxed at this point, so I didn't notice the narrow-dotted line wriggling through the water towards me. I only became aware of it as it wrapped itself around my hands, and its head appeared in front of me. His tiny pearly eyes peeked into mine, and his slithery, slit tongue kissed the air a few inches away from my face.

I froze right where I stood. The sweat started to pour again, but now it was cold. A tingly chill crawled up my spine, but none of that could make my eyes blink. The world stopped spinning for me as I stared at my death. It was slowly getting dark, and I wasn't sure if it was the daylight that was dying or my senses were failing me. And then suddenly, out of nowhere, appeared a pair of hands. In one swift motion, it grabbed the snake below its eyes, threw a cloth over it and pulled it away from my hand. The cloth was blue in colour, and it smelled very nice. That was all that I could notice as it brushed against my face. And then I collapsed face-first into the water.

I think I would have passed out for a few moments until I felt a tug at my arm. As I opened my eyes, I saw my saviour. Her hair shone like gold in the dying rays of the sun, and the blue of her clothes reflected on her dusky eyes. For a moment, it was like I was looking at that girl from the lake in the English countryside. Just like her, this girl had just saved my life. And I wasn't going to let her disappear."

Fernando suddenly stopped talking at this time. It seemed as if he paused for something. And it happened soon after. The silence of the night was shattered by a huge thundering sound not too far away. Another one followed soon after. The ground shook under its impact.

"What were those sounds? What just happened?"

"It means the night is coming to an end. And it is time for you to leave."

"But you didn't finish your story!"

"The story never ends. I just remembered that my bit got over a long time ago. You, I guess, were only supposed to be part of it until this moment!"

"I hate to leave things like this."

"You have got no choice. You must leave Damanpur before sundown."

"Yes, I know I am leaving. Horen will come for me early in the morning."

"No one's coming. And you can't wait either."

"What do you mean? Why?"

"I can't explain it, this is all beyond reason, but my instincts tell me so. And they are never wrong."

"But how do I leave on my own? The roads are blocked."

"You will find a map inside your bag, wrapped around the device you were trying to record my voice with. Of course, you won't find anything on it. I could have heard those wheels spinning from a mile away."

❋ ❋ ❋ ❋ ❋

There are times when we so intensely wish for something not to happen, that when it eventually does, we feel responsible for it. Maybe we waste so much energy thinking about it that we make it happen. Like, for example, in a game of Ludo when you take a hop ahead of the other player knowing well that he can kill your token if he rolls a four. All your instincts then get clouded in thinking about that one probable outcome that you don't want. And then when he indeed rolls a four, you are not sure if you should blame his sheer dumb luck or your own damn self for it. Something similar was going on in Nando's mind as he scampered through the bushes and fields in order to find a way out of the mess, he found himself in.

He decided to follow the route suggested by Fernando, although it sounded ridiculous at first. He had to leave the mansion from the backside by going over a wall. And then, after sneaking through someone else's courtyard and jumping across a muddy creek, Nando had managed to reach the beaten track as mentioned by Fernando. From there onwards, the journey was supposed to be simple, albeit arduous. Nando needed to follow the track until the point where it ended abruptly and bifurcated to the left and right. But he was not supposed to follow either. Instead, he would need to get off the road and continue straight across the empty farmlands. A few hours down that way should lead him to Chhatimpur. Fernando had told him that if he managed to reach there, he would find a way ahead.

He had actually used the word if, and Nando could now see why.

Even before he could reach the end of the beaten track, he found a group of locals blocking his way. There was no way to confirm which part of the tussle they belonged to. And Nando's appearance was so different that there was no way he could mingle his way through their lot. He was sure to catch their attention the moment he was seen. So, he quietly turned away and hoped to find another way to get across them from a distance without losing sight of the direction he was supposed to move in.

He managed to do that and, in fact, was able to find an almost parallel path to the tracks to move forward. But not for long. Soon he discovered that the road ahead had been decimated, and it was obviously a man-made effort. What made matters worse was that he could see police pickets on the other side, and they were preparing to get across to this side by using wooden planks as a makeshift bridge. So, Nando had to move away from there again, and this time, he ended up straight inside a village. He was afraid to ask anybody for help, but he knew he badly needed some help. The sun was blazing bright and shiny, and the heat was getting exceedingly unbearable. Thankfully, he noticed a lonely old man sitting under a tree with his goats by his side, so he approached him and asked him politely, "Can you tell me which way is Chhatimpur?" Surprised, he looked up at Nando and then waved his hand around and said,

"This is it". Now it was Nando's turn to be confused, and then he looked around as well. "Am I already there?" he thought, his hopes looking up finally. "Where are you headed?" the old man asked again. "Which way is the highway?" Nando responded with a question. "That way, across the canal." The old man showed his fingers to the east. "How far is it?" Nando asked again as he tried to make sense of the way. To that, the old man just waved his hand, making it obvious it would take a while to reach. "No worries," Nando told himself as he thanked the old man and got going with renewed enthusiasm. "Home is that way," he told himself.

Nando reached the canal sooner than he had assumed, and to add to his happiness, he found it barely held any water. "This shouldn't be an issue; I should be able to cross it easily." The place was quite empty, and he was thankful for that. He didn't want to attract any more unnecessary attention. He quickly took off his shoes and rolled up his trousers. He hung his shoes to his backpack when suddenly he heard a mechanical rotor whirring loudly somewhere nearby. Then there was suddenly a gush of fierce wind blowing in from the opposite bank, creating wild ripples in the water. Nando looked up in surprise towards the sky. There was a helicopter flying in towards him. It passed over Nando's head and went in the direction from where he came. And then he heard the other sound; the sound of a hundred people who were chasing the plane on foot and now flocked the other bank, cheering as if they were in a carnival. Soon people started to gather on this side of the canal as well, and before he knew it, the entire place was swarming. Nando looked up at the sky once again as he resigned to his plight and quietly sat himself down on the mud.

* * * * *

The Return

Nando managed to make his way back to Damanpur by afternoon. He could barely drag his feet forward by the time he reached. He felt like he would drop dead any moment, and that was not just because he was tired. It had more to do with the burden of his disappointments. He hadn't been able to complete anything with success since the time he had reached Damanpur. Neither could he fulfil the requirements of his project, nor could he get himself out when he really needed to. He felt so bitter he didn't even bother to take the detours he had taken earlier. Instead, he walked right across the empty road that led straight towards the doomed schoolhouse.

The helicopter had landed on the ground next to the schoolhouse, and people surrounded it like it was a monument amongst them. A junior minister had arrived along with his entourage to take stock of the situation. And along with him came a few journalists who were now trying to talk to the locals and understand the ground reality while their cameramen were attempting to capture everything they saw through their lenses.

The school building was now a crime scene and, as such, completely cordoned off by the investigating authorities. Police personnel stopped anyone from going close to the yellow tapes. But even from a distance, the place looked like a slaughterhouse. The stink of burnt flesh filled the air. Smoke still emerged from the rooms. Bloodstains littered the walls. Broken windows and doors bore witness to the carnage that it had to suffer.

Nando tried to stay as inconspicuous as possible while he looked at these scenes. He had only known the place for a couple of days and been there for a brief amount of time. And yet it pained him to see it in such a state. The same place was bustling with energy the day he had arrived, and it was fuming with rage the last time he saw it. And now it looked like a wreckage, a lost battleground. Nando continued to stare at it for a while before he turned away. It was then that he noticed Sumitra. She was sitting in a corner all by herself, nursing a wound on her head and trying to stay away from the cameras. Nando felt a little comfort at the sight of a known face among the mayhem. It was the same for her as well.

Sumitra was among those few who had survived the horror and lived to tell the tale. She was still in shock, shuddering at every sound around her. As Nando reached out to her, he could clearly see the pain and shock writ large on her face. Probably it was a moment of relief for her when she saw him, as she could finally speak what had been choking her from inside. "Mr. Ghosal refused to leave her alone. He said it was her fault she was dead, and he would make sure she got justice. So, he stayed with her body. And now he is dead too," she uttered in a hollow voice. That's all that she needed to say to be able to breathe easy and break down finally. She buried her face in her palms as she howled and cried while Nando quietly sat himself down beside her. There was nothing to ask, but she started talking about it anyway.

"Surjo left late in the evening, quite unwillingly in fact, to get some rest. He said he would go to the police to report the incident in the morning. He asked a few of his closest aides to stay on guard here for the night, and he also said there was nothing to worry about. He was wrong. They came like a pack of hounds, armed with sticks and rods and with their faces covered in masks. Nothing but their eyes could be seen as they stormed the building. Initially, we could not figure out what was happening, but then one of them shouted their intentions aloud. They wanted the girl's body, and they took it."

Sumitra stopped abruptly as her voice choked at this point.

"You saw anyone else after the incident – Bishu, Horen, Fatik?" Nando asked solemnly. Sumitra looked at him blankly and then quietly nodded her head sideways.

Nando gave her a moment before he spoke. "So, they came to destroy what they thought was the only evidence we had against them."

Sumitra remained silent, but she realised what Nando was hinting at.

At this point, their discussion was interrupted by a sweet, female voice. They both looked up together to find a girl, a reporter whom they had not noticed until then, who stood right next to them now.

She was lean and dusky, with piercing brown eyes and a brutally innocent smile. She wore a khaki shirt and a pair of jeans. Her hair was tied up in a bun, and her neck was naked, with the exception of an ID card that hung around loosely. Everything about her oozed confidence, and one look at her was enough to reveal that she meant business – she carried that oomph in her personality.

She held out a bottle of water to Sumitra and said, "I guess you need medical help." She spared but a casual glance at Nando as she spoke.

"I don't need your help," Sumitra snapped like an animal. "And I don't want to talk to you either," she commented bluntly to the woman.

"You won't have to talk," she responded gracefully. "You should still drink the water. You need it." She smiled and put the bottle near their feet before she turned and left.

They both waited a moment, watching her leave. Then Nando quietly picked up the bottle, took a sip, and held it out to Sumitra. "She was right about that. Drink some water." Sumitra looked at him and then quietly took a sip.

"Sitting here wouldn't help either. Why don't you go ahead and get that injury checked?" Nando mentioned calmly as he slowly stood up and prepared to leave nonchalantly. "You seem to be awfully impressed by what that girl had to say," Sumitra remarked with a tinge of annoyance as she closed the lid to the bottle and put it down. "I have faced and survived much worse." Nando smiled, but he didn't seem offended at all. He quietly picked up his bag, looking the other way. And then, without turning his face, he calmly uttered, "No, you haven't. None of us has. It's best to accept it." And then, he started walking away from Sumitra, leaving her aghast and astounded. She wasn't used to such rude responses, although she herself had dealt quite a few. But the tide had changed.

Nando marched along on his way to the mansion. Something was bursting within him, and it felt good. His mind was clearer than ever before. He knew exactly where he wanted to be and what he wanted to do.

But his chain of thoughts was suddenly interrupted by a tap on his shoulder.

"Wow, you walk really fast. I had to jog the last few metres to catch up with you." It was the same journalist woman

Nando had met moments ago with Sumitra. She spoke as if they had known each other for ages, without any kind of awkwardness or hesitation. But it was precisely the opposite for Nando. He barely managed to share a stupid smile and kept walking.

"So, what are you up to here?" the woman asked again, undeterred by Nando's ignorance.

"What do you mean?" Nando responded, pretending to be confused.

The woman smiled.

"Well, we both know you are not from around here. And you didn't come here with us, of that I am sure," she said plainly, sporting a poker face all along.

"So?" Nando responded with a defiant, single-syllable question.

"Seriously? Is that how you want to play it?' the woman asked sarcastically, as she stopped with her hands on her hips and an angry look in her eyes. No guy could walk away from that. Nando had to stop and turn around to face her.

"What do you want? Why are you following me?" Nando asked agitatedly.

"Because you were talking to that woman like she was your friend. It's obvious you know these people and also what's going on here, which nobody is ready to talk about. I have come this far for the news, and I can't go back empty-handed. So, I am asking for your help. Please tell me what you know." She spoke earnestly, letting go of all the attitude she had been carrying around until then.

Nando smiled a little and said, "No disrespect, Madam, but people won't talk to you because they don't know you, and they don't trust you."

"But you are not one of them. You can tell me right," she implored, sounding almost desperate.

"But I don't know you either. You didn't even bother introducing yourself, and you expect me to trust you?" Nando made no attempt to hide the sarcasm in his voice. "I am afraid in this case me and these people are on the same page – we would both like to be left alone."

The woman was left in utter dismay as she realised what the guy was saying was bitter but true. In her eagerness, she had made a mess of her approach.

Nando turned around and started walking, even as he heard the woman saying, "I am sorry. I guess we started on the wrong foot. My name is Aparna. And you are?"

"Gone," he uttered while waving his hand in the air, without stopping to look back. Aparna stood there, embarrassed, and angry, watching her only hope walk away from her.

Nando entered the mansion and quietly walked up the stairs. But there was another surprise waiting for him as he entered his room. It was like a storm had raged inside. Everything was either scattered or dismantled. Broken pieces lay around like debris. Nando took a moment to gather what might have happened. He jolted around to check the drawer – the disc was gone.

The realisation slowly dawned upon him that he was now exposed to the same threats as these people. His choices were now as limited as theirs. He slowly stepped outside and reluctantly made his way to the library room, where he knew an old ghost of a young English fellow was waiting for him with some cosmic knowledge and a boring story.

Just then, he happened to look outside while passing through the balcony. He noticed something and quickly ducked and crouched on the floor. It was Aparna. She was outside the gates and peeping inside inquisitively. "How did she get here? Was she following me?" Nando thought to himself. But that didn't matter. "That's one unrelenting woman," he uttered to himself as he waited there patiently for the next ten minutes for her to leave. It was almost dark by then, and chances of being spotted were less. Nando slowly stood up, stretched his arms, and made his way to the other side of the solitary wall.

* * * * *

"You are back, once again. I am confused how I feel about it."

"Trust me. I myself am still trying to figure it out."

"So, why are you back?"

"It seems all roads leading out of Damanpur are shut for me."

"You and I both know that's not the truth."

"Is it? You tell me then, what is the truth?"

"It's about a girl, isn't it?"

"Which girl?"

"That I can't say. There are more than one I can see, and each one of them has a story. But which one's holding you back, I can't say."

"It's always about a girl, isn't it? Even for you? What was her name?"

"Her name was Maya. She used to live in the outskirts of the village with her brother. It was just the two of them, as both their parents had died when they were very young. They belonged to a family of potters, and, while they were not entirely outcasts, neither were they allowed to mingle with the upper castes of the society. Their activities were supposed to be restricted within their own fraternity, but there were no others in that hamlet. Hence, she was pretty much on her own while growing up. Her brother chose to join the British army instead of following the family's legacy. He said that the royal army offered the only job in the country where people were not chastised based on caste.

He used to stay away for months, and Maya used to sneak out into the forest and spend her afternoons by the swamp. She said she felt more secure there than anywhere else, as people seldom came along this way. That is, until the day I came along.

We started meeting there quite often, and soon came a time when those few hours of our day had become the centre of our existence. We would be lost in each other when we were together. And the rest of the time, we would sit back in our solitude and reminisce about those moments of togetherness. Our days seemed to pace themselves differently when we were in each other's company. And the days when we couldn't see each other would pass in distress and agony. A time came when we both realised, we couldn't stay apart any longer. That was our happy time.

But the situation in the country was quite the opposite. Though we would get very little news of what was happening, one could very well sense the palpable tension in the air. Some random soldier in Barrackpore had chosen to pick up arms against the tyranny of his master and for his self-respect. And he had ended up killing himself in front of his entire regiment after putting a couple of officers to rest. The news reached civil society, and initially, it seemed to have little effect on our mundane routines. But this was just the calm before the storm, and what looked like an inconsequential incident triggered by the insanity of one man was actually the beginning of a wildfire that would spread across the land. The ranks of the army which wore the Union Jack would soon be up in arms against the dominion. Across northern India – Meerut, Delhi, Lucknow, Agra, Kanpur, everywhere – the native soldiers turned on their commanders. They looted, killed, and ransacked the establishments that housed the British. The English soldiers, albeit in command, formed a minority in numbers, got massacred or fled. Things got worse with every passing day. When the English royalty finally woke up to the situation and took notice, the damage was beyond repair. They realised that the entire empire was at risk and out of control, and all their attempts to contain the carnage had proved futile until then. Embarrassed and enraged, they committed all they had to crush the rebellion for good. In fact, they decided to make an example out of these Indian soldiers so that no one else, in any other part of their far-fetched dominion, would ever again contemplate the thought of a mutiny.

During one of these clashes, Maya's brother, Madhab, got injured. He limped his way back home and hid there so that the chasing British forces couldn't find him. He had conspired with some of his rebel compatriots to kill a few white men. Maya locked herself up with her brother to nurse him back to health. We couldn't meet for a long time, and she couldn't even come and explain the reason in person. She cried while she attended to Madhab's wounds, and he wouldn't even know that not all those tears were for him. I sent her messages, but none came back. I was sure that she loved me too much to stay away for so long. And so, ill thoughts started flocking my mind while I waited in vain near the pond. When she didn't turn up for a couple of weeks, I got so worried that I ended up visiting her house in the neighbouring village, which I promised I would never do. I was too much in love to worry about the consequences. Was she happy to see me? She was. But she was scared too as well. It wasn't going to go down well with the villagers that one among them was getting close to one of us. It's like they feared us, looked up to us, wanted to be like us and yet they hated us for who we were.

Slowly but surely, the medicines started to show effect, and Madhab began to recover his strength. However, I was sure that he would never be fit enough to serve in the army again. But I chose not to tell him that. It would only be a matter of time before he would find that out for himself. As the fate of the rebels became more and more obvious, Madhab's opposition to our relationship grew weaker. Though he was aware that the local people would not approve of it, he didn't care much about them. He deeply despised the hard-line caste-based society that theirs has become, and maybe somewhere, deep down, he was happy that he had a befitting reply to all their cynicism. Because no matter how much they dislike the proposition of a native girl of lower caste getting married to their masters, they would not dare oppose the Englishman. Especially not after they have witnessed the utter ruthlessness with which we crushed the rebellion. And Bengalis were known to be the timid and peaceful lot. We didn't expect them to react the same way the northern part of the nation did. We were wrong. It so happened that their pain point was entirely different.

We never realised when he had pushed the farmers over the edge. In his play, Nil Darpan, a prominent Bengali writer, Dinabandhu Mitra, depicted their plight in a manner that had never been done before. Even before the government could take note and ban it from being staged, it had been successful in showing a mirror to the people. Witnessing your own suffering through someone else's eyes was all the fuel that this fire needed. Two brothers in Nadia district kickstarted a rebellion, which soon spread across the length and breadth of Bengal. The farmers refused to grow Indigo on their lands. They started asking inconvenient questions and stopped cowering before their master's wishes. This was unacceptable to the government. Emboldened by their success in suppressing the sepoy mutiny, they applied the same ploy once again. Bolstered by the free rein given to them, the police and the military managed to crush the opposition with an iron hand. Their operation was headlined by the notorious hanging of the rebel leader, Biswanath Sardar, aka Bishu, who was a dreaded dacoit and had become a nightmare for the government and their loyal zamindars. However, that didn't end the rebellion, which continued in a passive, non-violent way until the authorities formed the Indigo Commission in 1860.

But this phase of unrest didn't go so well for us. It coincided with what could have been the happiest moments of my life. Maya had agreed to marry me, and my father had to give in to my insistence. But it didn't go down well with the peasants, who were already fuming over his support for the government in matters related to the rebellion. It was no longer just about their lands anymore. It became an issue of hurting their culture and sentiments. It was being portrayed that while my father had robbed them of their lands, I wanted to plunder their dignity, their women. Not one person remembered the times when I had helped and supported them, even at the cost of lying to my father for it. Neither did anyone bother to ask Maya what she wanted. They would rather have her dead than see her happy with me. I always felt what my father did was wrong, and people should not be allowed to treat others the way he did. But they proved me wrong. On a cursed summer evening, the villagers laid siege to my house. I crouched and hid in the barn in my backyard, holding Maya tightly in my arms. Maya was trembling in fear as her tears wet my shirt, but I felt nothing but rage. That day I felt that maybe these people deserved nothing better than what they got.

My father's hired henchmen proved loyal to the money they were paid and stood their ground, firm and steady even as hundreds of angry men surrounded our house. They carried torches and spears. They threw stones and hurled abuses at us. My father stood at the balcony, holding a gun with just one shot left. He refused to leave me behind, showing unexpected strength of character. Or maybe it was his love for me, which had always been there, but he wasn't around to show it more often. Whatever it was, it felt good. Such is the irony of life – the exact moment when so much love, unexpected and unaccounted, showered upon me, was also the precise moment when unrequited and inexplicable hatred ended my life.

But that night took away more than just my life. And hence I remain incomplete, even in death. And to this day, I remain cursed to wander timelessly among these rusty shelves, flipping through the worn-out pages of these books, unaware of what is that I am waiting for, or if at all there is something that awaits."

"Hmm. So, this is how you died!"

"No. This is how I was killed."

"What's the difference?"

"That I wasn't yet ready."

"Nobody's ever ready for death."

"But this is unacceptable to me. To die in the hands of these uncultured, illiterate idiots. They can't be the judge, jury and executioner of my life."

"But you had no problems loving one of them. Or was it just because you thought you owned her too."

"She was my one true love. Never again try to insinuate otherwise."

"And you were killed by people you had oppressed and tortured for years. Don't try to insinuate otherwise."

"Is it that simple? Then how about the girl whose death you witnessed yesterday. Who tortured her? And who killed her?"

"You knew about that, didn't you? Is that what you were trying to warn us about? Then why couldn't you help us save her? Wouldn't you have saved Maya if you had the means?"

"She isn't Maya. Nobody ever will be. And I am done helping your kind. Never again will I be so naïve."

"Then why did you bother sharing your long, tragic love story with me?"

"You seemed a bit more educated and a little less of an idiot."

"But I am one of them in this war. Make no mistake about it."

"You are right. This won't happen again. None will be allowed to step foot in this room again. And neither will you."

"Don't worry. I won't be coming back. But don't you dare try to interfere in the world of the living ever again. You are a dead man. Stay dead. Be happy among the pages of history where you belong."

* * * * *

The Turmoil

The morning presented itself in peculiar discomfort. Nando could almost vouch that he was dreaming, had the feeling not been so familiar. And as he opened his eyes completely, he realised he was indeed lying on a table for a second straight night. His back was aching, and so was his head. But there wasn't even a speckle of water to drink. And he knew he wouldn't get any unless he fetched it himself.

As he dragged himself and his belongings out of the hole in the wall, he landed right in front of Bishu, who stood there gaping at him in complete shock. But it wasn't easy for Nando to recognise him immediately. His dark equine face was swollen, with a blood clot along the corner of the lips. His eyes seemed to have gone an inch inside the dark circles that had appeared around them overnight. Bruises covered the visible parts of his upper body. He limped a little as he walked towards Nando, and it seemed that his shoulders had drooped permanently. Before the boy could ask him anything, Nando signalled him to remain silent and started walking down the stairs. Bishu followed quietly.

"Are you okay?" was the first thing Nando asked as soon as they reached the landing where they couldn't be spotted from outside. He was genuinely concerned. But Bishu seemed indifferent. He didn't answer the question. Instead, he asked Nando, "Why haven't you left Damanpur yet?" Nando felt his voice sounded a little different too. He responded, "That's a long story. I will tell you later. But what are you doing here?"

Bishu continued to stare at him without answering, and it slowly started to make Nando uncomfortable. After a brief moment of awkward silence, Bishu spoke again, "I was sent here to look for what you had left behind. But instead, I find you. I guess we will have to manage with that." Nando was surprised. It was like he didn't know this boy at all. Everything about him was changed.

Bishu didn't utter another word as he led Nando outside, ensuring nobody could see them. His movements were sharp, his signals crisp. He seemed to have become a soldier overnight.

They followed the route across the boundary wall, which Nando was already aware of, but he didn't make it obvious. On the other side, Nando saw Horen waiting with his van. Happy to see another familiar face, he smiled. But Horen didn't reciprocate. His face remained gloomy as he turned to look at Bishu. They exchanged a look of which only they knew the meaning. Nando turned and looked at Bishu, who quietly pulled out a black cloth from behind his shirt. He signalled Nando to put it on his head. Nando couldn't believe they would ask that of him, especially after what he had done for them. He looked at both their faces as they stood next to each other now. And they looked back at him like any other outsider.

* * * * *

Surjo's hideout was an old, abandoned temple outside Hasanchawk, a few kilometres to the east of Damanpur. Nando remembered that Horen had mentioned this place during the ride to Damanpur. It was said that this temple was built by a dreaded outlaw, a bandit named Raghu. He was a farmer before he took up arms against the zamindars and landlords of the region. His reputation grew far and wide when he single-handedly wiped out all the men of a family of loan sharks who were living off unjust interests levied on poor peasants. It is believed that after that incident, most of the zamindars and landowners mended their ways and stopped the atrocities on their subjects. Raghu became a messiah for the poor and a nemesis for the rich. His name would instil fear in the hearts of the rich and the corrupt. He built this temple with the wealth he had looted, and over a period of time, this place became known far and wide as a very holy place of worship. As per the norms of the day, animal sacrifices used to take place on every new moon night. Raghu was rumoured to have been so strong that he could behead a full-grown bull with a single swing of his blade. People from distant villages would come to pay their homage to Goddess Kali, and it was believed that all prayers made on that night would be fulfilled. The myth spread far and wide, till one night, in the middle of the ceremony, the British government cracked down upon them. The crowd dispersed and scooted while Her Majesty's police force hunted down and killed each and every of Raghu's men, including him. There were no survivors. Since then, nobody ever came back to this place. The jungle reclaimed what was originally a part of it, with the exception of a few broken walls and pillars, and nothing but an old, faded idol remained, bearing witness to the changing times and tides.

Surjo had a similar expression of shock and confusion on his face when Nando arrived at the hideout, followed by Bishu. Horen stayed outside. Nando was happy to notice a few familiar faces like Mandar, Fatik, and a few others. And he noticed that the recent events had taken a toll on almost all of them, but Surjo seemed the worst affected. His eyes revealed a sense of discomfort and restlessness. He was now forced to lay low, and he wasn't used to that. But he knew his turf. It was not going to be easy for any agency to track him or catch him unless they had a mole amidst his men.

"How come you are still here?" Surjo asked the same question that had been coming Nando's way since morning. But Surjo didn't wait for any reply. He immediately turned to Bishu and asked, "Did you get it?" Bishu slowly shook his head sideways and walked away. Nando could literally see the disappointment descend on Surjo's face as he quietly sat himself down on the floor. Nando was now slowly realising how important the content of that disc had become, especially since the victim's body had been lost. And he was equally surprised by how little these people knew about digital data.

"I hope you guys are all aware that I do have the footage on my laptop. I can always make you another copy if you want," Nando stated categorically as he looked around at all the stooping faces surrounding him. Everybody looked up. This little bit of information seemed to give them hope. Information that Nando couldn't believe they didn't know already. He also couldn't believe that he was capable of doing something that gave people hope.

And this seemingly little thing brought back the adulation that had gone missing from their behaviour. Surjo's smile became welcoming once more. Bishu ran to get him a stool to sit on. But before he could sit and relax, he jumped to his feet at the statements that followed.

"We are back in business. Now we have the proof as well as the girl. We can trade. They have to give Sumitra back, and we will make sure to find the people who did that to us. No one will be spared." Surjo's voice sounded aloud among the walls, prompting enthusiastic reactions from almost everybody present there. Nando was the only exception, as far as he knew.

"What girl? What trade? And what happened to Sumitra?" a bewildered Nando dumped his entire list of questions at one go.

Nando would immediately regret asking those questions because what he would learn was no less than a nightmare. Sumitra had been arrested by the police for rioting charges as a key conspirator. A few others had also been taken into custody to Kolkata for interrogation. Kusum's body had yet not been recovered, and the police had started a witch hunt for the rest of the folks as well. In fact, they were planning to announce a reward for anyone with information about them. But that was not all.

The worst of the surprises was still waiting for Nando, one which almost made him jump out of his skin. Because at the back of the temple, among the ruins, sat a woman with her mouth gagged and her hands tied to a pillar. She looked distraught and dishevelled but Nando had no trouble recognizing her. It was Aparna – the journalist from yesterday. Nando stood there petrified as the girl looked up and saw him. She seemed more angry than scared.

"What is this? What is she doing here? And why is she tied up? Nando asked nervously. But nobody else seemed to be much bothered.

"What do you think? She is our hostage," Bishu mentioned casually as he walked up and leaned against the pillar across the corridor.

"Have you people lost your minds?" Nando now shouted out aloud, completely aghast at everybody's callous expressions. "Don't you realise how big of a crime this is?"

Nobody was expecting Nando to react so strongly. In fact, it was more of a reprimand. Surjo wasn't used to this, and definitely not in front of folks who idolised him. And least of all, from a nerd who couldn't imagine half the things he had already done. Surjo was vexed.

"What were you thinking all this while? That you were in a carnival or a drama show? We have been literally putting our lives on the line for the past so many months, and now we are left with no other but this. They have taken our right to protest, now we are going to challenge their ways of rule," he argued vehemently.

"By indulging in crime? Is that your answer? Then you are just proving them right by behaving exactly the way they said you would. They have been trying to brandish your rebellion as unlawful, and now you have validated that. It doesn't matter how legit your demands are if you ask the wrong way," Nando responded with almost equal anguish.

Everybody else remained silent, as a war of words enraged between the old pals, whose ideals seemed to be contradicting at this point.

"So, what do you suggest? We just sit here and do nothing while they keep coming after us until there's none of us left. Or should we just wait and hope for them to have a change of heart and forget about our friends they have in custody and who they might be torturing at this very moment for every bit of information they have?" Surjo asked.

"Of course not. What they are doing is wrong. What has already happened is also wrong. And we have the proof. We can take it to the people. And that girl that you have got there in chains could have been your weapon. Or at least someone else like her, who could have taken your message and your story to the people," Nando replied.

"And what would people do, support us in interviews? Stand in solidarity? Or maybe even observe two minutes of silence when we are dead?" Surjo remarked sarcastically and then continued. "We don't matter to them. They don't know our plight, and they don't understand our fight. We are just news to them. They are outsiders."

"You know your nonsense theatrics might work with these idiots, but not me." Nando's voice and temper had now risen to a level he didn't know he had. "You keep calling them outsiders when in reality you adore them and mimic them. And the only reason you loathe them is because of how badly you want to be like them."

The tone of their exchanges were slowly spiralling down as their tempers continued to flare up.

"What do you mean by them? You mean you, right? You are an outsider who just walked in, enjoyed our hospitality, lent a toy and now feels entitled to have an opinion about what we should do and how we should do it? Brother, you are here because you were of no value where you come from. And you have nothing to offer here as well," Surjo said the words without flinching a muscle on his face.

"Fair enough," Nando uttered after a brief pause, his voice cold as ice. "But you know what, brother? You don't own this place. And you might have a bunch of stooges following you blindly, but I am not one of them. I came here because I wanted to. I helped you because I could. And I will leave when I feel I am done. Because without me and my toy, you have got nothing. You can sit here and watch the leaves rot till the agencies come looking for her and you. And that day, I will be there, just to look you in the eye and tell you how worthless your efforts have been."

An uncomfortable silence followed, with the two friends staring into each other's eyes before Nando turned to leave.

"You can't go." Surjo's voice echoed from behind him. Two of his guys immediately flung themselves in front of Nando, blocking his way.

The situation seemed to be going out of hand with no one senior enough to intervene between the two of them.

More specifically there was no one Surjo would care to pay attention to.

"So, now what? You are going to kidnap me as well. That's your genius plan." It was Nando's turn to unload sarcasm. "And then what? You are going to torture me, for every bit of information, for your right to protest?"

Surjo continued to stare at him, his eyes filled with rage, while Nando stood facing him in stoic silence, breathing unusually loud.

There was a muffled voice that interrupted their standoff at this time. It was Aparna trying to attract their attention.

"See what she needs," Surjo ordered, without moving from his stance.

Bishu quickly walked up to her and removed her gag. She let out a big breath and then said, "I have been trying to say this for a while. I think I know someone who can help in this situation."

* * * * *

It had gone completely dark and quiet by the time the group had finished discussing their plans. It wasn't safe to travel anymore, so both Nando and Aparna had to stay back among those ruins that night. They finished the meagre meal that Horen had fetched. And then the few trusted men went off about their business, leaving the two of them by themselves with a couple of blankets. They could not light any fire for fear of getting spotted, and it indeed got cold around there at night. Right next to the ruins was a dirty old swamp with nothing but murky water about a foot deep and home to nothing apart from mosquitoes and leeches. And the stink was barely bearable. The two of them crouched with their backs to each other, leaning against a pillar that bore signs of decay all over it. Right next to them lay the stairs leading to the marsh, and it was obvious that they hadn't been used in years. They both knew it was impossible to get any sleep, and they had nothing to say to each other either. They but it wasn't meant to be.

At around the middle of the night, Nando felt a restless hand tugging at his blanket near his right shoulder. He turned around to find a visibly petrified Aparna, clutching at his neck while pointing out at the swamp with the other arm. Nando turned his head to check out whatever she wanted to show. And what he saw was enough to amaze him.

The Prussian blue night sky, with the exception of the stars that glittered all over its expanse, had laid a cover of darkness over everything that existed around them. Nothing moved. Nothing could be heard or seen. Nothing, except occasional, bright green balls of fire that erupted from the muddy waters and faded into thin air, like a spirit leaving the earth in a hurry.

Everything around would light up for a moment in its flare, and then the darkness would return to devour it all back.

"Relax, do not be afraid," Nando spoke in a gentle and calm voice as he put his hand on hers. "It's just a will-o'-the-wisp. It's quite a common sighting in the rural parts during this time of the year."

Aparna immediately pulled back her hand and tried to conceal her embarrassment by looking the other way. Nando now sat right next to Aparna, with their contours brushing against each other. Nando felt he should say something to lighten the uneasiness that ensued between them.

"You know, Horen was saying that some people actually believe that the damned soul of Raghu still lingers around and haunts these premises. Many people claimed to have seen him, and they were not all drunk. I wonder what you would do if you happen to spot him now, given the fact you almost ripped my blanket at the sight of a stupid fire bubble," he quipped.

Aparna looked at him in veiled anger, and Nando heaved a sigh of relief. The ice was finally broken.

"Do you actually believe in these ghost stories?" she asked mockingly.

"I wish I didn't have to," Nando murmured softly as if speaking to himself.

"What do you mean?" an astonished Aparna exclaimed with a smirk.

"Nothing, I was just asking what's your take on it?" Nando countered her with both a question and a smile, thus shrugging off the momentary awkwardness and the thoughts that led to it.

"My take! I would prefer a ghost any day over the people we live with," Aparna retorted with a wry smile, much to Nando's surprise. He somehow couldn't relate the idea of unhappiness with this smart, stunning, successful woman.

"Wow, that's a lot of anger on the living beings. Is it just what you have seen here or do you have reasons of our own?" he asked in a sentient voice.

"What do you care? You are just a random guy whom I have met at work who seems to be stuck in the same mess as I am." Aparna suddenly snapped back, completely breaking out of character and the situation. Her face turned a shade darker while her eyes seemed to light up for a brief moment. Maybe there was a raw nerve hurting somewhere within her that gave way to this venom.

On the other hand, Nando was quite literally jolted, so much so that it took a while for him to register that she had just insulted him for no fault of his. Once he overcame the initial shock, he felt a sudden surge of anger gushing through his veins. It was unlike anything that he had felt before. A primal and pure animalistic urge for retribution began to cast over his senses. But somehow, he managed to control himself and uttered, "Good to know it's just men who repel you, not the entire human race. Thank God for that, but an early heads-up would have saved us both a lot of trouble." Having said that, he tried to get up and leave. He didn't know it, but that was the bravest thing he would have ever done. But halfway through, Aparna grabbed his hand. She didn't pull him back, neither did she let it go – she just held it firmly until Nando sat himself back. She hadn't looked at him since she had made that comment. They continued to sit like that, without saying a word, for what seemed like a really long time. A couple of more will-o'-the-wisps appeared during that time, adding some momentary spectacle to their otherwise uncomfortable company. She sat looking at it like it was magic, hand firmly in hand with Nando, who was busy looking at her as if she was magic too.

And then she spoke.

"Sorry about what I said earlier. I would really like it if you continued to keep me company," she said.

"And why should I do that?" Nando asked sarcastically.

"Because I am yet to thank you and knowing myself, it might take a while. And you need to hang around until then," she responded with absolute authority, which seemed to come naturally to her. And then, without giving Nando a chance to respond, she asked again, "So, what was it about this spirit you were talking about? Do you think it's still there? What do you think it would have done to us if it were to appear right now?"

"It would probably ask you if you can actually accomplish all that you said earlier," Nando asked indifferently, his voice still sounding grumpy.

"What do you mean?" Aparna asked, finally turning to face him.

"I mean, you made quite a few tall promises to Surjo – to find and free Sumitra, to garner media attention to this struggle, and even get the judiciary involved. Can you really achieve all of that?" Nando asked calmly.

"I wouldn't have committed if I wasn't sure that I could deliver," Aparna answered confidently.

"But how are you so sure?" Nando asked, visibly surprised.

"Because I know some powerful men, who owe me some favours" Aparna uttered in an indifferent voice, turning her face away once again.

"And I suppose these are the same men that had made you bitter about all of us?" Nando asked softly, intending not to annoy her again.

"Most of them, not all, I guess. You seem decent enough," Aparna responded jovially this time.

They both smiled.

"Is that the thanks you made me wait for?" Nando asked casually.

"No, that wasn't, this is," she exclaimed as she leaned forward and kissed him on his cheek. Nando's face reddened, but thanks to the dark, Aparna seemed not to notice as she continued to speak. "It was quite brave what you did back there, despite barely knowing me. What made you vouch for me?"

"Well, somebody had to," Nando answered shyly.

"What are you doing here anyway? I mean, in the middle of this chaos in this godforsaken place?" she asked.

"You will probably laugh at the irony if I tell you," Nando quipped.

"Try me," she said with a smile.

Nando sighed and then began to speak. "I am training to be a soil scientist. I know you probably wouldn't even have heard of this profession, but I assure you it's a real thing. We research different soil types, and you would be amazed at what we can find and predict based on it. And that's what brought me here."

"That's it? I mean, you got yourself in this mess just for doing that," Aparna asked, with an unmistakable sense of surprise in her voice.

"What do you mean by that? This is important work I am doing. I know it doesn't sound fancy, it doesn't offer a big pay or perks, some people might think it's not even respectable enough! But I value my work. And that's all that matters to me." Nando reacted sharply, in a manner that didn't come to him naturally. But Aparna could sense the unease with which he uttered those words, so she tried to tone down the conversation.

"Hey, I didn't mean it that way. Of course, what you do is important, and yet I am sure that there are many others like me who are not fully aware about it. It's just that when I saw you in the middle of all this, I guess I kind of assumed you would eventually reveal yourself as an undercover agent or something like that," Aparna answered cheekily, with a broad smile. She knew how to use her best weapon at will.

Nando responded just as she would have expected of any guy. He smiled back and said, "I am sorry that I reacted that way. I guess I have just gotten used to people looking down upon my job, or maybe my decisions and choices. I guess they measure value in an entirely different way. But if I succeed in doing what I am here for, then everything will change."

"What exactly are you planning to do?" Aparna asked with genuine curiosity.

"I wanted to analyse the soil samples of this terrain and suggest, based on scientific data, whether we could improve the production capacity of these lands or would it be more beneficial for everyone if it fetched more value as an industrial plot. This one study could have resolved the issue for good, and the outcomes would have been indisputable. This could have been the most important breakthrough of the year and could have paved the way for more such assignments at other parts of the country facing similar conundrums. But all of those possibilities seem to have gone up in smoke now, and so has my chance to prove my worth to my family." Nando tried to elaborate his intentions as best he could but unconsciously drifted towards venting his frustration in front of a complete stranger who seemed to be interested.

Aparna waited patiently for him to finish. She didn't fret or get frisky but simply continued to stare at his face, even though Nando failed to reciprocate during most of the conversation.

"Okay, you were right. That's funny, in a sad kind of way." She finally broke the silence after allowing Nando a moment to gather himself once he was done talking.

"So, now what?" she asked again as Nando remained silent.

"I need to wait until you fulfil your promises and come back to Damanpur with some good news," Nando finally responded.

"And what's stopping you from leaving before that?" Aparna asked.

"Maybe I can, but it doesn't feel right when I think about it," Nando said.

"Do you think it's safe for you to stay here?" Aparna asked again, with a tinge of nervousness in her voice.

"I honestly don't know anymore," Nando answered plainly.

They had almost run out of things to talk about, so they kept quiet for the next few minutes. They were both cold, scared, and uncomfortable. Morning was still a few hours away. Then, Aparna slowly placed her head on Nando's shoulders and whispered, "I would suggest you rather not...but..." Nando didn't let her finish and completed the rest of it himself, "but there's no other way." The rest of the night passed away quietly as they dozed off for the last couple of hours before daybreak.

The next morning as she left, they said their formal goodbyes. Everybody around still seemed to be sceptical about the both of them, and they knew it wouldn't change until she showed results. As Aparna boarded Horen's van to leave, she gave Nando a parting smile and said, "You know there is a word for it, but I can't seem to remember it now."

"Word for what?" Nando asked.

"For you, for what you are doing here," she said, and then she left, leaving

* * * * *

The **Reckoning**

A few minutes later, Nando made his way back to the mansion. Nobody, including Surjo and Bishu, bothered to check with him or offered any help. And Nando didn't mind that either. He was no longer in a state of mind to reason with people who wouldn't understand. The best thing was he didn't even feel lost or helpless because of it. He felt absolutely comfortable getting his own food and water and then going back to his room all by himself.

But he no longer wanted to risk living in that room. Firstly, it was in a mess after being ransacked. And there was every chance that the culprits could come back again to finish the job. He didn't want to go back to the library either, that he was absolutely sure about. So, he decided to temporarily find an uncharted corner somewhere among the ruins at the back. He needn't be afraid of ghosts anymore, and for the animals, he was carrying precautions with him. He had come prepared for his fieldwork, which meant he carried all necessary items for spending nights outdoors. He had to scout for about half an hour before finding a relatively solid pillar towards the far end of the property, completely hidden from any outside eyes. Most of it remained intact and held together with a part of the roof, which seemed undamaged as well. He decided to pitch his makeshift tent underneath it. The day had almost ended by the time he finished preparing for the night. As he tucked himself in his bedding and switched the small halogen lamp to read a book, he assured himself, "This should all be over in a couple of days."

As he roamed around among the bushes the next morning, he remembered that this was the same place Bishu had mentioned, where his friend Moinul had died. The place did match his description. But maybe because Nando was not in the same mental space as Bishu and Moinul might have been, he didn't feel anything exceptionally spooky about the place. He was more worried about the living people who were either depending on him or hunting for him.

For a change, Nando took a bath by the well, pulling up buckets of cold water from the dark depths of the underground and splashing it over himself from the top of his head. He felt fresh and alive. He breathed better. Life becomes a bit easier when one is no longer anxious about the unknown. He walked up to the small eatery at the end of the road, ordered and ate to his heart's fill. He continued reading throughout the day; even collected some samples he thought might prove useful once he was back in the laboratories. Only a matter of time, he kept telling himself. And that soon turned out to be true.

Aparna came back a couple of days later. Nando was so thrilled to see her that he rushed to her and took her hands, cupping them warmly within his own. She had kept her promise, something which Nando was desperately hoping for but wasn't entirely sure would happen. But there she was, looking charming and confident as always, as she handed over the editorial published in the most popular daily in the state. It bore testament to the fact that she had outdone every expectation in delivering on her commitments. The news covered in detail on how the central government had taken cognisance of the situation and reprimanded the state authorities on its plans and actions. The fact that the local opposition was in power at the centre also aided in this. The matter had now escalated, and the Governor had proposed a neutral and high-level SIT probe into the matter. But that was not all.

A notable number of eminent intellectuals have also come out in support of the cause and had mobilised a mass movement within a span of just two days. And at the forefront of this movement were the acclaimed filmmaker Sulogna Mallick, noted painter Suddhasattva Basu, and the young heartthrob of the movie-goers Kuldeep Bakshi. They had organised a candlelight march to protest against the atrocities reported in Damanpur as well as the alleged state-sponsored terrorism looming in this region. They have also kickstarted a nationwide campaign to gather support and have submitted a memorandum to the President himself, requesting his intervention in the matter.

However, she had saved the best news for the last. With a broad smile on her face, she took out an envelope from her purse and handed it over to Surjo as she announced, "Sumitra is being released today. She should be in Damanpur in another hour and a half."

This last bit of information was like the cherry on the cake. Everyone around erupted in joy. This was way more than anything they could have asked for.

"Why couldn't she just come with you?" Nando still managed to ask.

"If we want to get justice as per law here, then we need to follow the rules more often than break it. I interviewed her while in custody, so it would have raised a few eyebrows if she had come here with me. That was way too much even to ask," she explained the nuances the best she could.

"It's simply unbelievable how much you have accomplished in this short time." Nando voiced his thoughts once he got an opportunity to walk with her where no one would see. He had been meaning to spend some alone time with her when she got back, just the two of them, to pick up where they had left off the other night. Aparna smiled as Nando continued, "I can still understand the rest, but getting such support from the celebrities and the Page 3 fraternity, that's got to take some work. Kudos to you!"

Aparna stood silently as Nando spoke the words, watching a couple of kids fishing in the pond with a small net. A few seconds passed quietly before she realised that a response was due. She turned to Nando, who was now engrossed in reading the minute details mentioned in the newspaper, and spoke casually, "actually, that was the easiest part. Celebrities are looked up to be the face of our society, and they are supposed to be the voice of people in times of crisis. Also, a few of them keep looking out for such issues to voice a sensational opinion in order to stay relevant and add weightage to their credibility. So, all I had to do was brief them about the situation."

Nando replied casually, while still occupied in the article, "but I am sure that even reaching out to these people must need a herculean effort. A few years back, I happened to be visiting one of these parties where my father was invited. The chief guest for the evening was none other than the superstar Nirmal Kumar himself. I saw him speaking very generously to my father and a few other dignitaries. But in spite of idol worshipping him for most of my teenage years, I couldn't even manage to utter a single word when I was in front of him. But then again, that is just me, and you are a journalist. You are supposed to be smart and approachable and..."

"And a celebrity's daughter," Aparna abruptly interjected Nando's ranting.

"Sorry, I didn't get that" a visibly surprised Nando asked.

Aparna replied with a smile, "I just said that apart from being a journalist, which is how I like to introduce myself, I happen to be a celebrity's daughter as well. And though I can't really claim any credit for that, the fact remains that it does work in my favour in some assignments, so I thought you might want to add that to the list."

Still confused, Nando asked, "So, you mean your father is a film star?"

"No, not my father. It's my mother. I am Sulogna Mallick's daughter," Aparna replied calmly, looking into his eyes as she spoke.

Nando was so surprised at this revelation that he couldn't speak for the next couple of minutes. Aparna waited patiently while they both contemplated their versions of the discussions that were about to follow.

Nando was the first to speak.

"Actually, I read something...before coming here...I guess it was in a magazine or something..." Nando mumbled, trying to frame a question that wouldn't sound rude or intrusive.

"About Kuldip and my mother, right?" Aparna asked indifferently.

Nando remained silent.

"Do you remember what I told you the other day? Some powerful people owe me favours. How does it matter who they are or how they are related to me, right?" she asked once again, though looking the other way this time.

They fell quiet again. And this time for good. Maybe both of them waited for the other to say something. But neither could come up with anything. So, they quietly waited for Sumitra's arrival.

But, close to three hours passed by, and there were still no signs of her. Every passing minute began to add to their nervousness. Surjo walked around anxiously while Nando and Aparna sat thinking about other possibilities. Their brains were now running faster than their hearts, trying to figure out the puzzle. It was Nando who finally spoke when his thoughts had started to collude, and Aparna pitched in to fill the missing pieces till they were finally able to get a complete picture of the grim reality. But not before every grain in their faith had been tested.

"Do we know for sure if she was released from prison as per the plan?" Nando asked.

"Yes, she was. My colleague Abir had picked her up outside the jail and he made sure she was on her way to Damanpur," Aparna updated as much as she knew.

"But she hasn't reached yet. It couldn't take her this log. So, where did she go?" Surjo enquired impatiently.

"Maybe we can go and check at the highway bus stand. If she had arrived, somebody would have noticed," Nando suggested.

"If she had reached the highway, she would already be with us," Surjo stated confidently.

"Well, unless she is in some kind of danger," Aparna said.

"No harm can come to her in Damanpur. It is perfectly safe here now. It's all in our control," Surjo exclaimed, his tone angrier this time.

"We had thought that earlier as well," Nando uttered nervously.

Surjo turned around and looked at both of them, one after another.

"How about the possibility that something might have happened to her in the city? How confident are you that your colleague has done what he is saying? Why are we just blindly believing him?" Surjo asked agitatedly while looking at Aparna.

"I know him, that's why. He is a good friend and I trust him completely," Aparna responded with equal ferocity.

"But here's the thing, I don't know you that well. You came here on your own for your work and then had a change of heart. So, you then decided to help us by doing an interview which, again, is just your work. You were the last one to have met her. So, I think you are the one whom we should be asking the question – where is she?" Surjo now spoke in a shrewd, cold voice that left his listeners in a state of shock. Aparna didn't know how to respond to that. It was Nando who spoke up.

"You cannot be serious, Surjo. She is the one who delivered whatever hope we have of getting justice for Kusum. Why would she come back if she was guilty? And why do you keep doubting her?" Nando retorted sharply.

"Why don't you tell me why you keep supporting her? How come you trust her so much by knowing her so little?" Surjo now unloaded his frustration on Nando. It seemed like a do-over of their earlier stand-off was inevitable until Aparna intervened.

"Will you guys please stop doing this over and over again?" Aparna shouted, throwing them both off their guards. "I am here because I want to, and I am helping because I feel I should. You don't have to believe it if you don't want to, and you don't need to justify on my behalf either," she said while pointing her fingers first at Surjo and then at Nando.

"Can we now please focus on the issue at hand?" she spoke again after a brief pause, after making sure that her audiences were done with their silly debate.

Then she quietly pulled out a note from her bag as she continued to speak, "This is the note I had received from my colleague Abir, who was chasing this issue. He knows these things better than anybody I know. He ensured all the formalities were completed. And then he was supposed to escort her until Aramu. Sumitra had said that she can manage from there."

"Yes, that's what any one of us would have done," Surjo now spoke, confirming the decision. "She could have easily found her way from there on her own. The question is whether she reached there or not?"

"Well, I am sure you can find that out. Like you said, it's all in your control." Aparna quipped with an obvious taunt directed at Surjo.

Surjo looked at her annoyingly and uttered, "Yes, I can." And then, without indulging in further banter, he quietly signalled someone outside to get the information. Aparna didn't bother to check who that was or where he went.

Nando had remained quiet all this while. He now asked Aparna, "Was Abir aware that you would be coming here today?"

"No, I didn't mention this to anyone. I didn't think anybody needed to know about my personal plans," Aparna responded, surprise evident on her face and in her voice.

"So, even if Abir had anything to do with Sumitra's disappearance, he would have no reason to believe that you would come to know about it, at least definitely not so early," he uttered calmly, without making any eye contact with her while he spoke. And then he looked straight into her eyes.

"And why would he do anything like that?" Aparna asked coldly.

"To get a few powerful people to owe him favours, maybe," Nando responded in a similar tone, without breaking eye contact.

"And to put him up to this task would be…?" Aparna said, her voice fading as she spoke as she tried to come to terms with the possibility, and so Nando had to finish the sentence. "That would be the very same people who had helped you get her released in the first place."

Surjo listened to this conversation closely as he felt a morbid sense of glee about being proven right. But that bubble broke almost immediately as the man tasked with fetching Sumitra's information entered the room in a hurry.

"Sumitra was seen in Aramu by our folks about an hour ago," he blurted out in a hurried voice. He probably didn't even notice the way Surjo's face changed colour as he spoke.

"Then where is she? Where else could she have gone? Who is supposed to man the highway entrance to Damanpur?" Surjo's voice thundered in desperation.

"It is usually done by Das babu. He is our eyes out there, has been for a while now," somebody else replied.

"So, go check with him. If Sumitra had reached Aramu, there is no way she wouldn't be in Damanpur by now." Surjo immediately tasked the man.

"But his cabin has been closed since morning." It was Horen's voice this time. The mostly silent man has finally spoken. "Even the farmers complained he wasn't there to pick up his regular supplies today" added someone else from the group.

Surjo slowly sat down on the stairs as the truth started sinking in. It wasn't like he collapsed, but his shoulders had drooped for sure.

"That doesn't make any sense. He has never done that before. Unless..." he didn't bother finishing that sentence.

"Unless a man who had once been driven from his home had again been threatened with the same," Nando uttered softly.

* * * * *

The Farewell

The next few moments were of haste. Once Surjo realized they had a mole amongst them, one who had been a part of their inner circle and almost every discussion, he understood how exposed and vulnerable the entire operation had become. Each of their names and hideouts had been compromised. And now that the opposition had Sumitra, it wouldn't be a surprise if they decided to strike again. After all, they still needed the footage and all its copies. And they wouldn't hesitate to go to any extent to get their hands on it.

"You are coming with me this time. It's all over. Just a matter of time before they coerce Sumitra into telling them who you are and where to find you. You are not safe here anymore," Aparna uttered anxiously, as Nando continued to stare at her blankly. He was still struggling to come to terms with what he himself had helped them infer.

"Don't you think we should make one last attempt to save Sumitra before we leave? Doesn't she deserve that?

And anyway, if these people are really who we think they are, how safe will I be anywhere in this state?" Nando uttered dejectedly.

"But what can we do? All this is way out of our league. It was stupid of us to think that we could make a difference. Nothing we do will ever matter," Aparna blurted out as she put her hands on her head in desperation.

"Yeah, I guess you are right. We probably can't make a difference, but at least we can try being someone different. Right?" Nando exclaimed calmly.

Aparna looked up and stared right into Nando's eyes.

"What are you thinking?" she asked nervously.

"I have an idea. As long as I have that footage, they will surely have to come to an agreement if we so demand" Nando uttered confidently.

Aparna didn't say anything. Instead, she gave Nando a cold, hard stare.

Nando, however, chose to ignore it as he divulged the plan cooking in his mind. "If we somehow manage to send them a message and propose an exchange – one where they release Sumitra, and we give up the footage in return, maybe they will agree. I mean, they have to agree. Why shouldn't they? That way, they could get what they want without any more trouble."

"And what will you achieve out of it? The entire rebellion is falling apart right in front of our eyes. Even if they give up Sumitra today, don't you think they can come after her again? Or, for that matter, they can come after any or all of us. How will you stop them if you give up the one piece of evidence that we have?" Aparna asked.

Nando remained quiet for a moment as he spared a quick glance around him. She was right. And what she said made absolute sense as well. But then he said something to which Aparna didn't have an answer.

"If nothing else, at least she will live. She will live to fight another day." Nando uttered softly.

Aparna sat quietly for a while before she picked up her stuff and prepared to leave. Then she turned around and said, "I will put a note outside Das babu's cabin on my way back. I am sure they will be keeping an eye on it. Where do you want them to meet?"

"Mention the mansion. I will take it from there," Nando confirmed confidently.

"Okay," she said curtly and prepared to leave.

"I know you must be thinking I am a real fool for doing this, right? But you tell me honestly, after all that we have seen and heard, can you really blame me for trying? Even if there is the slightest chance of saving a life, shouldn't we give it our all?"

Aparna finally smiled as she turned and looked at him. And then she replied, "Yes, no and maybe." Nando took a second to decode the pun, and then they both laughed out loud. It was no assurance, but Nando felt good. "So, you are not going to stop me from doing this, right?" Nando quipped again. Aparna replied with a warm smile, "I am not going to try."

They walked together for the next few steps without saying a word. Before she hopped onto Horen's van, who had been patiently waiting for her all this time, she looked around one last time as if to soak everything in. Then she looked at Nando and uttered softly, "Be safe. See me when it's all done." Nando quietly nodded and kept looking as Horen steered the van away. This goodbye felt harder than the last one.

*   *   *   *   *

Nando came back to the mansion, alone and anxious. The torment that he had wished for so long to be over was finally coming to an end. And it seemed like he had a role to play in the final act as well. He was confident the culprits wouldn't waste any more time once they got the information about the tapes. And they would surely come prepared. Nando knew he had to be ready for the encounter. So, he did the best way he could. His plans were quite elaborate. He tried to replicate what he could recall of similar situations that he had seen in a movie. He really hoped it would work but honestly had little confidence about it. When he was done, he packed his bags and belongings, except the original copy of the tape. He wrapped it in a plastic cover and kept it in a nook where it couldn't be found unless directed. Then he covered his face with his anti-dust mask and took refuge in the farthest corner of the mansion, among the ruins. And then the wait began.

The sun set at six. And the temperature started dropping soon after. It was usual in these parts. But the weather otherwise seemed gloomy that evening. The wind was missing. Soon, a thin layer of fog started to settle in. The entire mansion remained steeped in complete darkness, with the only exception of the streetlamp outside the gates, which kept flickering on its whim. This was to Nando's advantage. He kept his eyes fixed at the entrance, sparing a quick glance at his watch every now and then.

They arrived around eight-fifteen. It was all so quiet that Nando could hear the revving of their car engine from hundreds of metres away. It was a black SUV. Five men stepped out, including the driver. Sumitra wasn't among them. Nando had considered this possibility. His first assumption had been proven right.

He quietly picked up a bamboo shoot that he had gathered earlier in the day. It served his purpose to perfection. He put his mouth at one end and started barking instructions in the heaviest possible voice he could conjure. The men were startled as a hollow voice echoed from the darkness in front of them.

"Stop there. Bring Sumitra forward."

The men had no chance of guessing where the words were spoken from, not just for the way the voice sounded but also because of the dense mist that hindered their visibility. But they still tried. They pulled out their torches, and barring one person, who seemed to be their leader, the rest dispersed around the area. One of them hurried upstairs inside the main building while two others darted towards the row houses. One of them wandered into the back but didn't dare enter the bushes. He stood there, nervously flashing around his torch, which proved to be of little help to him. Nando watched him acutely from his hideout, barely a few feet away. They were so close that he could almost feel the man's fear and hesitation as much as he felt his own.

After a few tense moments, Nando was relieved to see the man turn back and leave while nodding his head sideways. Soon the others joined him. Nando let out a quiet laugh. His plan seemed to be working. They now had no option but to do as he wanted them to. And they realized that as well.

The leader now signalled one of the men, who slowly walked back to the car and pulled out a woman with her hands and mouth tied. It was impossible for Nando to identify her from that far away. But he had a plan for that as well. First, he asked them to untie her. They reluctantly complied. Then he again put his mouth to the bamboo conch and shouted, "Sumitra, if that's really you, reach the door to the dead man's office. Nobody else moves."

He knew that an outsider wouldn't know who he was referring to, but Sumitra would surely understand that he meant Pramod Ghosal's office on the right. The men weren't keen to let her go, but they knew they had little choice. Their leader reached into his pocket, pulled out what seemed like a firearm, and aimed it at her. And then they watched as slowly started moving forward.

The smog was getting thicker with time. Her steps were hesitant, as she didn't know whom to expect on the other side of it. It took her a couple of minutes to cover those few yards. The men behind continued to keep a hawkish eye on her and everything around.

Nando was relieved to see that the woman was headed in the right direction. Once Sumitra was at the door of the house, Nando spoke again, "Follow what you find at the bottom of the door." Sumitra slowly stooped, and she had something in her hands when she stood back up. Nando had already tied a rope there that would lead her right to him and out of reach of the goons. Nando was elated that his novice plans were getting the desired results. But, suddenly, at that very moment, the calm of the night was shattered by a flash of light followed by a huge bang. "She isn't going anywhere until we get the footage and all its copies," the leader's voice thundered in the emptiness. Nando thought for a moment. Nando knew he couldn't carry on with this caginess for long. He felt he shouldn't push his luck anymore. Sumitra would be out of sight of those men in another few steps.

And the men wouldn't risk staying for long once they got what they were looking for. Especially now that they would have gathered attention by the gunfire.

Nando pondered for a moment and then spoke once again, "Stop shooting and listen to me. First, put the gun back in your pocket. Second, the moment I say where you can find what you are here for, Sumitra starts walking." He waited for a moment to see if the gamble paid off. It did. The leader put the firearm back in his holster, or so it seemed from a distance. "This is it, no more games" Nando told himself. He took a deep breath and started talking again. "Turn to your left. There is a hole in the boundary wall there." He paused for a moment to check if Sumitra got the cue and started walking. Much to his relief, she did. So, he continued again, "get to the other side of the hole where the land descends into the river. You will find a lone cotton tree there, with a bag tied to its upper branch. That bag has all the footage you are looking for. I have no other copies." Nando had deliberately tried to make the process cumbersome to ensure it needed more than one person to accomplish it. Because he needed to buy as much time as he could for Sumitra. He honestly had given up all copies of the footage and everything related to it in that bag. He wanted all of this to end now, once and for all. He really wanted to get over with this chapter of his life.

As the men scurried in a bunch towards the wall, Sumitra had already stepped into the misty darkness at the back, well out of their reach. She hadn't been able to spot Nando yet, but he watched her closely as she slowly approached his hiding place. The men weren't paying much attention to her anymore, apart from their leader, who still stood stoically at the gate. He moved his head from time to time, passing his glances all around the place. Once his men confirmed they got the bag, he pulled out a huge torch from behind him and flashed it at the back to see if he could still see the girl. But Nando was sure that wasn't possible. The fog was too thick. The light beam dispersed mid-air halfway across the courtyard. But it did increase his heartbeat for a brief moment, though. He knew well enough that if the men had planned to conduct a thorough raid, the fog wouldn't be able to save them. But before the leader of the gang could plan anything further, a commotion arose among the men outside the wall. He turned the light as well as his attention towards that, giving Nando the required window to get Sumitra's attention. He swiftly pulled her behind the pillar where he hid, but he remained anxious about what might have caused the ruckus.

The next set of events unfolded so fast that it didn't allow anybody any time to think or plan their response. As the commotion outside the wall abruptly ended in a couple of painful cries, suddenly something flew in from the hole and hit the leader, throwing the torch off his hands. He let out a loud grunt at the initial impact but quickly managed to get over the pain. However, using that window of distraction to its advantage, something darted in from behind the wall and jumped on the man, attacking him with brute force and a blunt weapon. It was a frail, dark figure, and the streetlight was enough for Nando to identify the assailant. It was Bishu.

Nando was completely stumped as he witnessed the scuffle in utter shock and awe. The stupid, young teen he had met a few days back was almost unrecognisable now. The soft, jovial fellow was gone. The person he saw now was possessed, enraged, and unhinged. It was sheer hatred that gave him the audacity to tussle with a much stronger opposition. Nando feared for his life, but at the same time, he was mesmerised by this transformation. Maybe that's how an anarchist is born, he thought in his mind. You take away one's love, and you have yourself a demon.

The David vs Goliath war, however, didn't go as per the fable. Bishu was soon seen lying on the ground, with the leader now towering above with his gun in his hand. His accomplices had also joined him, though it was obvious that they had been hurt in the ambush. But Nando noticed that one of them had still got the bag. "Enough of this nuisance. First, I will kill this joker, and then I am coming for you," the leader declared angrily as he stared into the dark void where he knew the girl and her saviour were still hiding.

"You will do any of that" suddenly a voice was heard from their close quarters. It was so unexpected that everybody shuddered upon hearing it. Nando found it familiar, but before he could take a guess, the men had already spotted the speaker, who now stood a few feet away from them. Nobody saw him coming, and there was no place for him to come through. And yet he was there. He stood with his hands locked behind his back, with no sense of alarm or tension. Nando knew this person all too well. Nando looked on flabbergasted as the leader of the gang, now pushed beyond his limits, raised his gun, and pulled the trigger without any warning.

Nando heard the bang; he saw the flash and yet the figure remained unmoved as the bullet went right through him and hit the wall. The men were baffled, and then immediately after, fear descended on their faces. Nando couldn't believe what he was seeing.

Shrouded in the mist, a few feet away from the goons, stood Fatik, wearing a wily smile on his face. The same Fatik, whom Nando had met so many times, in the middle of the day and amidst many other people. "All this while…he…he was…" Nando's stream of thoughts was interrupted as another voice sounded out of nowhere. "He is right. Your guns wouldn't help you anymore." Nando looked on in complete bewilderment as the mist around the men suddenly started to cluster and take human form until their identities could be clearly recognised. This voice was familiar too. Pramod Ghosal's spirit still wore the same smile he sported when he was alive. "None of you will be spared" a female voice arose from behind the men now. They all turned in unison, their hands shaking and feet trembling. Nando couldn't see this figure, but he could hear Bishu's nervous voice as he shouted, "Didi… you are alive?"

"No, brother," the voice spoke again, "but I am here."

Nando and Sumitra felt like their feet are cemented to the floor, and time had stopped moving ahead in their lives. It was hard to tell if they were still a part of the living world or if they had been transported to a twilight zone between realms. The only thing they knew for sure was that they were still breathing and yet witnessing an unbelievable saga unfold in front of their eyes.

The men were now scared beyond their wits, surrounded by dead people who were awake and who couldn't be hurt by any weapon they carried. The spirits had called out their warnings, and now they stood calmly, looking at the men to decide what to do. The leader, who was obviously the smartest and strongest of the bunch, also seemed to have lost his nerve at this unthinkable turn of events. Bishu was still on the ground, but he sensed the opportunity. He quietly scampered out from among the men and then quickly got back on his feet and started sprinting towards the back of the mansion, where Nando and Sumitra were hiding. The leader was jolted out of his trance at this sudden development and, almost out of habit, took out his gun and shot at the boy, twice. Bishu fell on the ground with a howl, but it was drowned in a spine-chilling cry that arose from among the dead who were present. It was like a war cry. And then they were joined with another voice, a strong, angry familiar English voice, as the figure slowly walked down the steps of his mansion among his compatriots in death.

> *And that slaughter to the Nation*
> *Shall steam up like inspiration,*
> *Eloquent, oracular;*
> *A volcano heard afar.*

> *And these words shall then become*
> *Like Oppression's thundered doom*
> *Ringing through each heart and brain,*
> *Heard again — again — again –*

Within a matter of seconds, the fury of the fallen unleashed hell upon the living. The sky thundered, and the winds blew amuck. The overhead cables to the streetlight suddenly snapped, and a blanket of darkness descended upon all. The men lost all control and started firing in unison and in all directions, even as the war cry of the dead echoed among the living.

Nando's eyes were already accustomed to the darkness, and he wasn't new to the company of the dead. So, he quickly crawled out of his place, even as Sumitra tried to stop him. He could see Bishu lying on his face a few feet away, and he couldn't just let him die. He needed to know if he was still alive and if there was still a chance of salvaging something worthwhile from this mayhem. As he reached the boy, his body felt cold. He nervously put his hand to his face, and finally, he could smile.

Bishu was still breathing. But he would need immediate medical attention to survive. Amidst the random gunfire, the unruly weather, and an army of angry dead people, he tried to pick up the boy and take him to safety. He knew it wasn't going to be easy. He was right. A couple of steps, and he felt something sharp and hot bite his back. The pain blanked his mind immediately, and the next moment, he was lying with his face to the ground.

* * * * *

The **Destination**

It was almost daybreak when Nando opened his eyes. The sky was getting clear, birds were chirping, and the wind was cold and mellow. He was still lying on the ground, and Bishu was lying next to him. As his memories came rushing back to him, he hurriedly put his hand on the boy's face. Much to his relief, Bishu was still breathing. As he sat himself up, he noticed Fatik standing along the corner, like his usual self. The other dead folks couldn't be seen around anymore. That included Fernando. Maybe he had gone back to his books in the library room, Nando thought to himself.

"We need to get going. The police will have a handful to deal with today," Fatik uttered as he walked towards him, while pointing his fingers at the gate. The place was ridden with random bullet marks, bloodstains, and a couple of dead bodies. They were the goons who seemed to have been killed in their own crossfire. Suddenly, Nando remembered Sumitra and spontaneously turned to look where she was hiding. The place was empty.

"She is safe. She went to get help for Bishu," Fatik spoke again as he seemed to read Nando's mind.

Nando now turned and looked at Fatik. He stood right there, like always, like he was real. Nando could see him as clearly as he had seen any other person in his life. And yet he wasn't. He was a dead man. And there were others like him. They worked together. And even Fernando seemed to be in cahoots with them, even though he claimed to hate everybody around here, irrespective of whether they were dead or alive. None of it made any sense.

Nando sat there grappling with his thoughts for a while, unable to figure out what to say or ask. It took him almost an entire minute before he could come up with the first right thing to say. "Thank you for your help last night" he uttered as he finally managed to pull himself up from the ground.

"Well, we didn't have a choice. One of our own had reached out." Fatik said as he turned and looked at the farthest corner of the ruins. A young girl stood there chatting with Pramod Ghosal. "That is Kusum, right?" Nando asked. Fatik quietly nodded his head. Nando continued to look at them for a few moments before speaking again. Then he turned towards Fatik, looked him straight in the eye, and asked, "So, all this while, have you always been dead? Even when we first met at the schoolhouse?"

"Yes," Fatik replied with a wry smile on his face.

"Then how come some see you and some don't?" Nando asked curiously.

"I guess only a few choose to see us in the light. And in the dark, we choose the few who can" he replied with a naughty smirk.

"So, you mean anybody can see you during the day? Then why don't they?" Nando asked again, intrigued by the seemingly stupid concern.

"I honestly don't know. We have always existed among the living, but yet only few have noticed us, even when we were alive." Fatik answered in a grim voice.

They both fell silent again at this time and turned to look at the ruins where the ghosts of old man Ghosal and a young Kusum slowly started to disappear in thin air even as they remained engaged in conversation.

"Everybody deserves a chance to save the ones they love," Fatik uttered at that moment, as if to himself.

"Bishu will live. I am positive. There has to be some light at the end of this long, dark tunnel." Nando sounded stubbornly confident as he spoke.

"That's it. That's the spirit I think made it possible for you to see me, or the others, irrespective of who we were or what we wanted. But then again, maybe that's what got you into this mess to begin with," Fatik quipped plainly.

Nando finally managed to smile for the first time in a while. And then he uttered sourly, "I understand you, maybe I would understand the others. But what about Fernando? He behaves like an obnoxious prick, and yet he comes to our aid, and he continuously warned me about the future. I really can't figure out what goes on in his mind."

Fatik could sense Nando's confusion. He smiled and said, "You need to understand that he has been dead for more than a hundred years, so he doesn't always follow what's going on with us."

"Then how did you convince him to help you? He seems to hate us all," Nando asked curiously.

"Well, this is his property, and anything happens here, you can't leave him out of it. Actually, I should be thanking you for choosing this spot for your little adventure. We sure needed his help," Fatik uttered with a shrug.

"Well, that makes sense. If there's one thing I have learnt over the last few days, it is that there is no limit to how far people will go to protect what they claim to be their own," Nando answered rather seriously.

"Isn't that true. What we call our own makes us who we are. Otherwise, what would you even live for?" Fatik spoke in a philosophical way.

"And do you think Fernando thinks of you as his own? Do you believe it's even possible?" Nando asked warily.

Fatik remained quiet for a few moments observing Nando keenly, and then exclaimed, "he knows he is one of us now, whether he likes it or not."

"What do you mean?" Nando asked.

"It's simple. We are the dead. There is no longer any black or white among us. There's no then and now. But we are still human. We understand that we are a marginal community that needs to stick together to survive. Actually, it's the living who seemed to have forgotten this fact," Fatik exclaimed with a tinge of sarcasm in his voice.

"The dead talking about survival, isn't that ironic?" Nando responded in a bemused tone.

"Yeah, I can see how it would seem funny. You see, we are the past. We are part of history in our own ways. Survival for us means not being forgotten, to be able to stay relevant, to matter, if we can," Fatik explained in a more sombre tone this time, "and if we are forgotten or ignored, the past will come back to haunt. Then we will see a Moinul being fascinated by the same things that Surjo used to chase, or a Fernando trying to find as a man what he fancied as a boy. Or for that matter, we will have a Swarajnagar trying to revisit its glory days by uprooting its own people."

Nando didn't know what to say anymore, so he remained quiet and they both continued to look around them. It seemed surreal for both the dead and the living to look at the remains of a war. It was Nando who spoke first.

"So, what happens now?" he asked Fatik.

"Nothing new. The living will carry on with their way of life, and the dead will go back to existing in obscurity," Fatik uttered indifferently.

"And what about the revolution? Will it survive? All the evidence that we had is gone," Nando asked, a bit sourly, as he looked at the bag lying near the gate. It was burnt and torn into shreds, and the contents shattered to pieces.

"Evidence doesn't fuel a revolution; emotions do. As long as there are people who feel the cause is just, there will be always be a soldier left to fight. And if this revolution is destined to die, then there will always be another," Fatik exclaimed.

"And what about me? Where do I go from here?" Nando finally managed to ask, putting aside his hesitation.

"You know you are one of us now, right?" Fatik asked with a smirk as he pointed his fingers at Nando's dead body lying next to Bishu's unconscious self. It was slowly turning cold and blue. Nando looked at it dejectedly, and then he shrugged and said, "Yes, I can see that very well."

"You died trying to save a local lad, so I guess you belong here now. You just need to find a place of your own, and then you will be okay. The dead need a home too," Fatik said as he put his arms around Nando's shoulders.

"Really? So, who stays where?" Nando enquired as they slowly walked towards the gate, realizing that the day had got brighter and people would be up soon.

"Well, Fernando, as you can see, stays in the mansion, in his favourite library room. He is a bit moody, doesn't like to step out very often. And I don't think he would like to share his space either," Fatik said as he rolled his eyes.

"Who said I would want to?" Nando said grumpily as he turned to have one more look at the first-floor balcony. It seemed empty as usual. "But maybe I will visit him sometime later," he murmured this time, after a brief pause. He couldn't figure out if Fatik heard it, but he didn't respond.

Instead, he continued to comment indifferently, "At least we get this much freedom. We get to choose where we belong, and for our own good reasons. Mr. Ghosal has chosen to reside at the schoolhouse, and Kusum stayed back in the post office building."

"And what about you?" Nando asked.

"I prefer staying on the open road. That's why you might see me around more often than others. I guess these guys will join me." Fatik said casually as they passed by the dead bodies on their way to the gate. Their souls were still stuck in their corpses.

"Isn't there a distinction between friends and foes after death?" Nando couldn't help but ask.

"No, buddy, death dilutes all distinctions. In fact, I happen to know a couple of them already, and not in a pleasant way. But we have all the time to figure that out now." Fatik chuckled and winked as he said those words.

Nando looked at him in surprise and then looked at the corpses. He might have had more some questions creeping into his mind, but he chose not to ask. It didn't matter anymore anyway.

They kept walking until they reached the gate, and right before stepping outside, Fatik turned and asked Nando, "So, what do you think? Where would you like to be, now that you can be anywhere?"

Nando pondered for a moment as he looked all around himself, and then said "there's only one place around here where I have some good memories and an unfinished story. I think I will stay there – in that old, abandoned temple by the stinky marsh where Surjo used to hide," he said in an assured voice.

"Well, our lives are nothing but an episode in an unending saga, so no matter where you leave…some stories will always remain unfinished. But you do realize you are proposing an insanely radical thing, right?" Fatik uttered.

"You mean a ghost in a temple! I know that's not supposed to happen, but then we are not supposed to exist at all, remember? We are not even supposed to have a conscience, or a conversation, for that matter." Nando answered with a smirk.

"Well...uhm...I..." Fatik mumbled for a bit, as he seemed unsure of how to speak his mind, maybe for the first time since they had met. When he finally managed to put words to his thoughts, he said, "I hope you understand it's not going to be an easy task. The living would be offended. Their age-old beliefs would be shaken, their sentiments would be hurt and faith will be tested."

"So?" Nando asked vehemently, in a tone unusually aggressive for him.

"So, I would suggest you rather not, but...who cares, right?"

* * * * *

www.ingramcontent.com/pod-product-compliance
Lightning Source LLC
Chambersburg PA
CBHW021528150726

47990CB00006B/2137